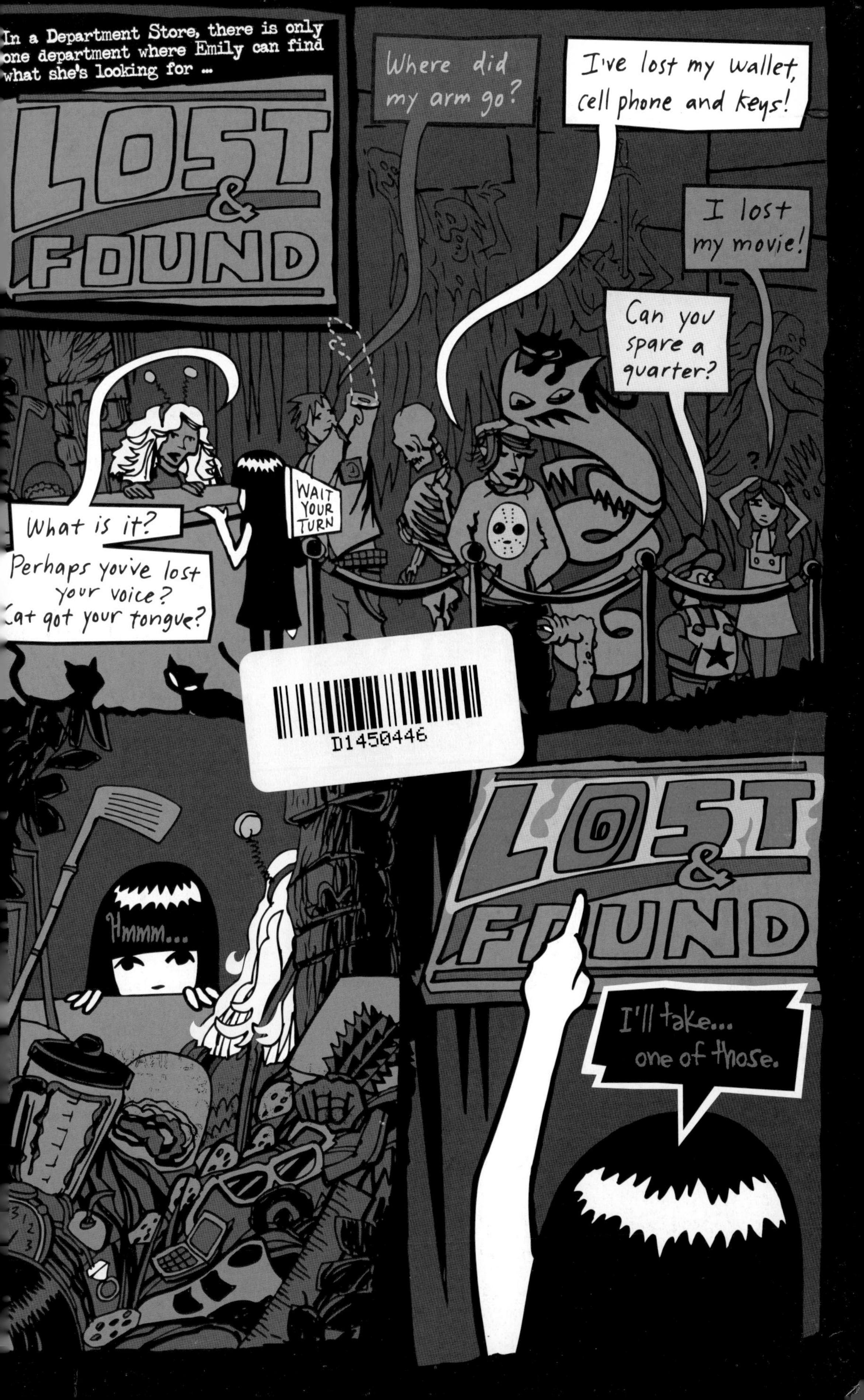
In a Department Store, there is only one department where Emily can find what she's looking for ...
LOST & FOUND
Where did my arm go?
I've lost my wallet, cell phone and keys!
I lost my movie!
Can you spare a quarter?
WAIT YOUR TURN
What is it?
Perhaps you've lost your voice?
Cat got your tongue?
Hmmm...
LOST & FOUND
I'll take... one of those.

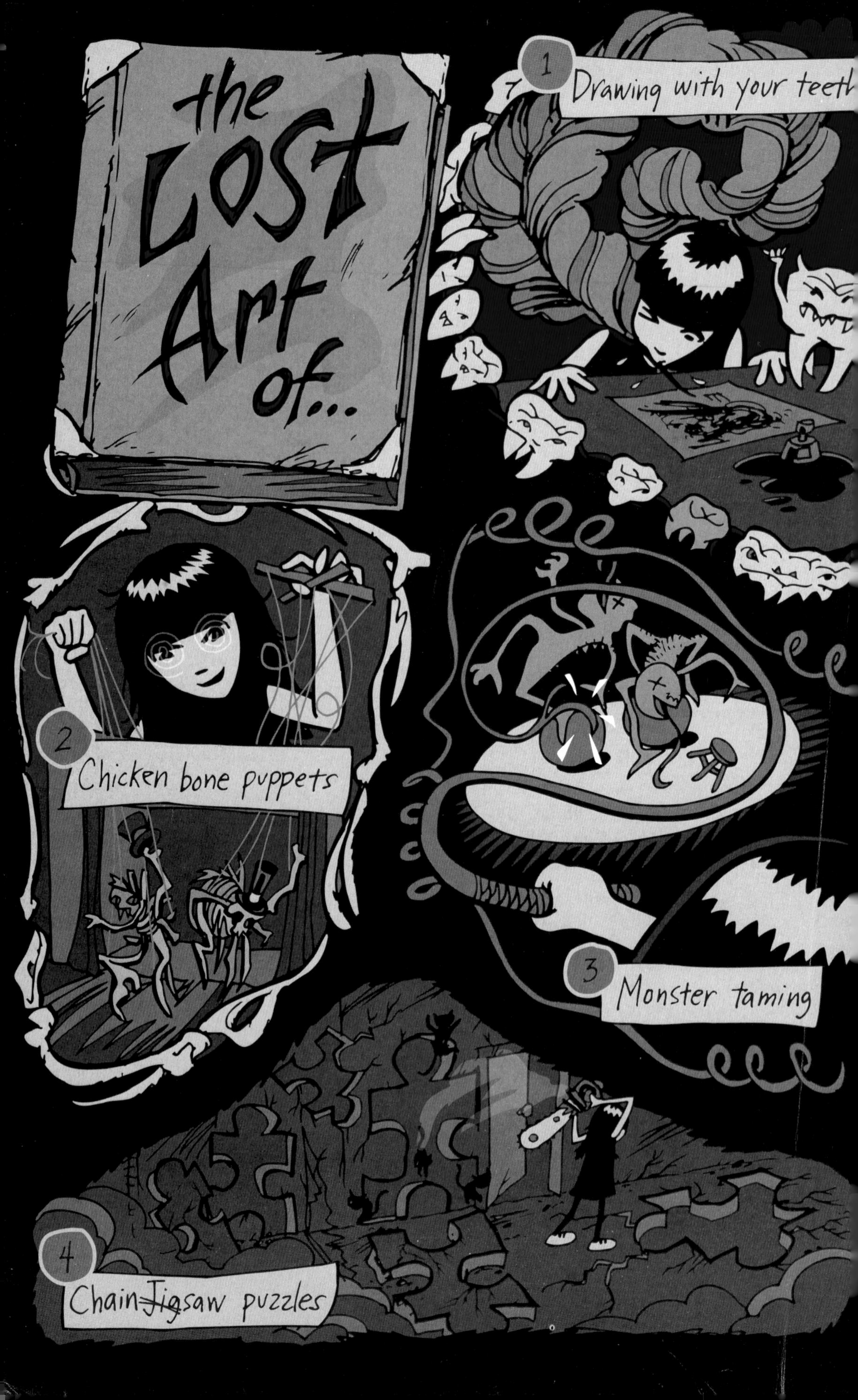
the Lost Art of...
1 Drawing with your teeth
2 Chicken bone puppets
3 Monster taming
4 Chain ~~Jig~~saw puzzles

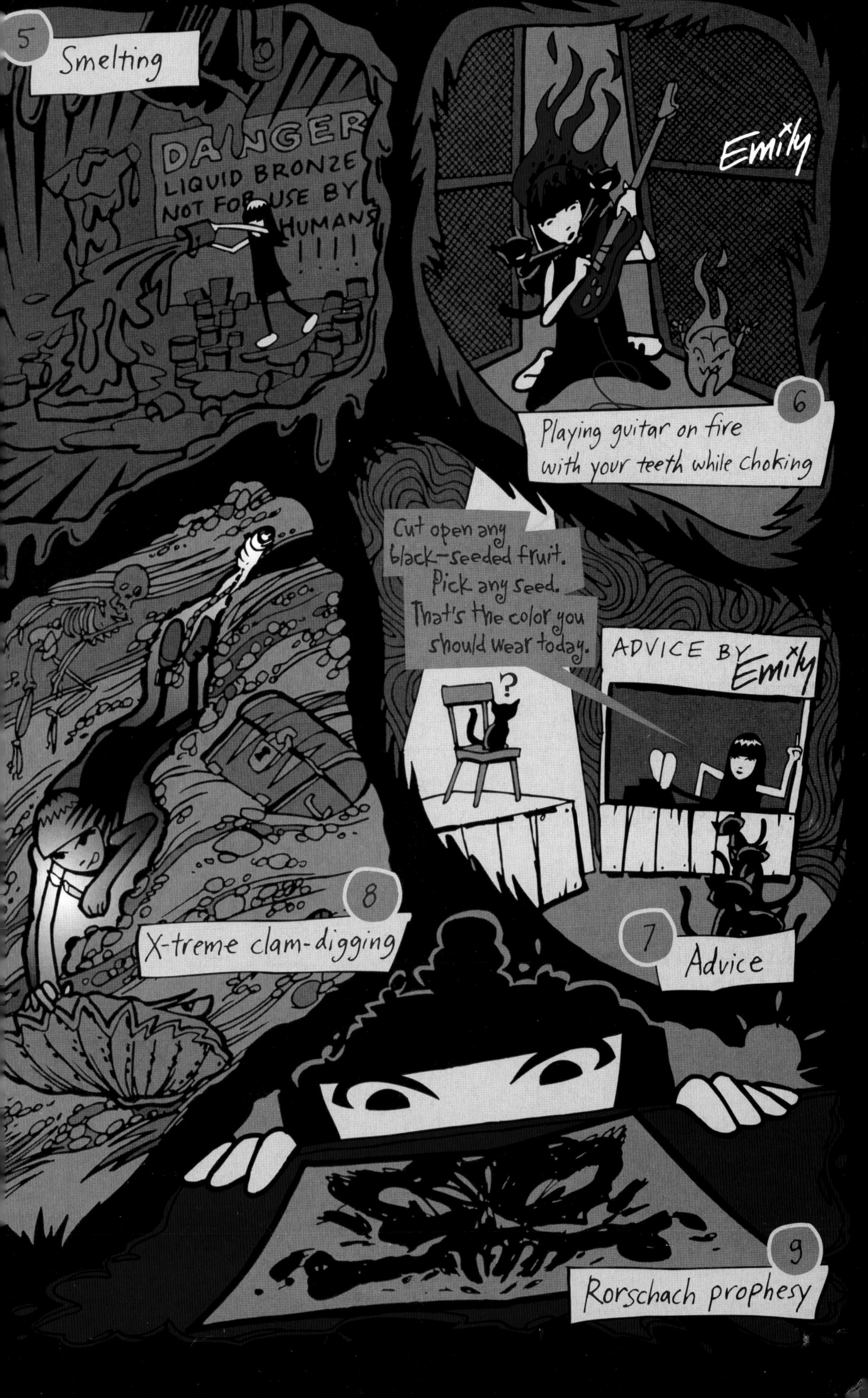
5
Smelting
DANGER
LIQUID BRONZE
NOT FOR USE BY
HUMANS
!!!!
Emily
6
Playing guitar on fire
with your teeth while choking
Cut open any
black-seeded fruit.
Pick any seed.
That's the color you
should wear today.
?
ADVICE BY Emily
7
Advice
8
X-treme clam-digging
9
Rorschach prophesy

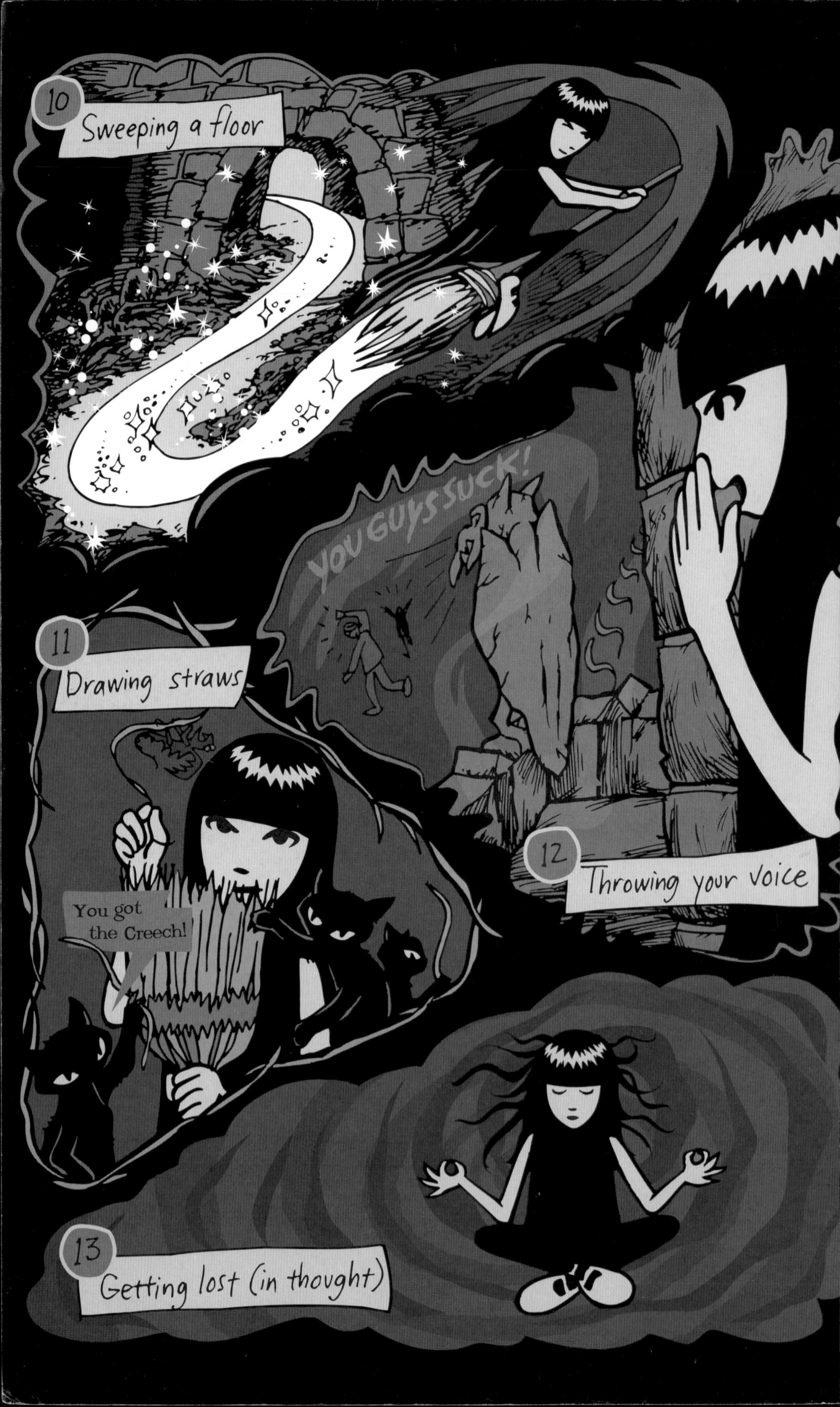
10
Sweeping a floor
YOU GUYS SUCK!
11
Drawing straws
You got the Creech!
12
Throwing your voice
13
Getting lost (in thought)

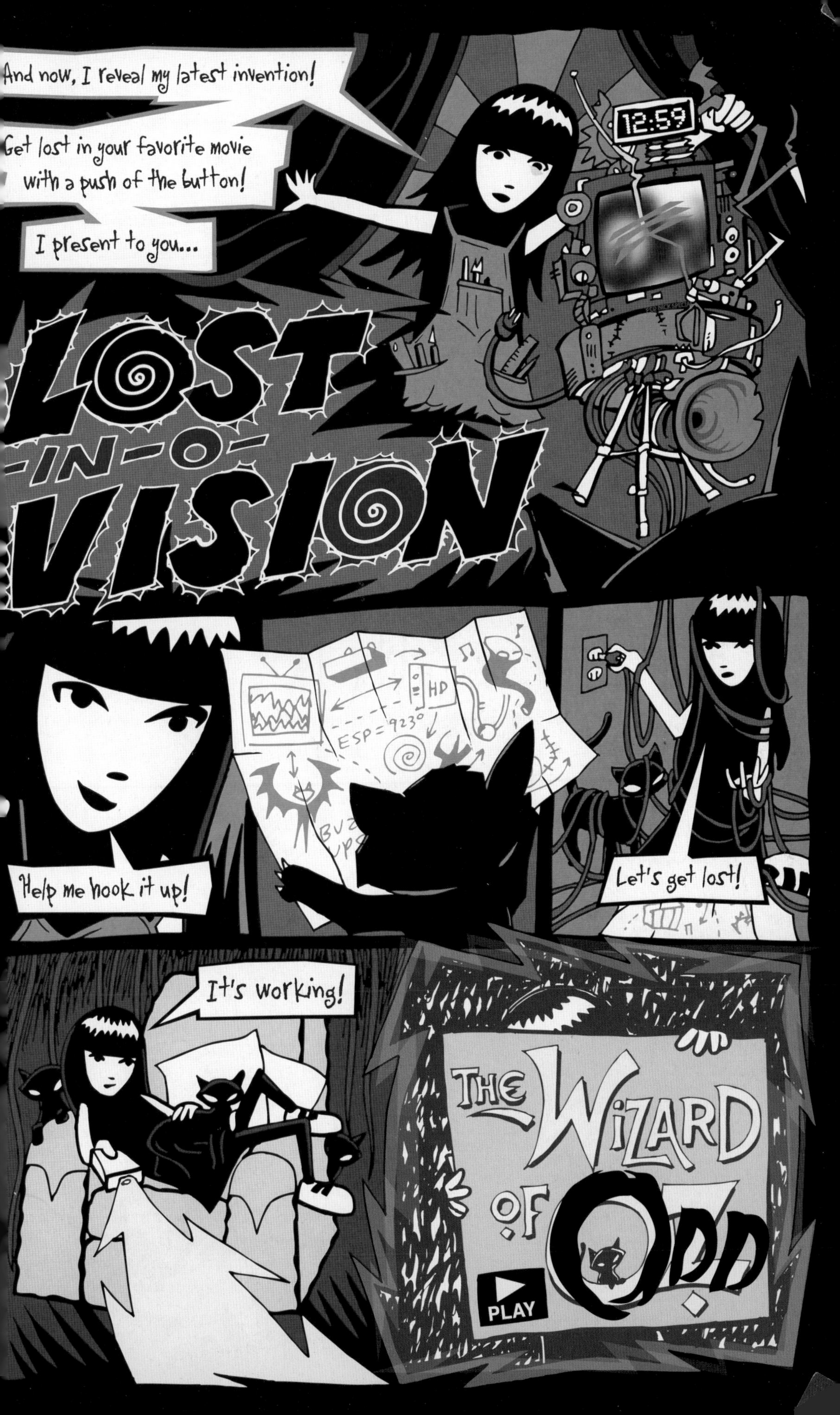
And now, I reveal my latest invention!
Get lost in your favorite movie with a push of the button!
I present to you...
LOST -IN-O- VISION
12:59
HD
ESP=9230°
Help me hook it up!
Let's get lost!
It's working!
THE WIZARD OF ODD
PLAY

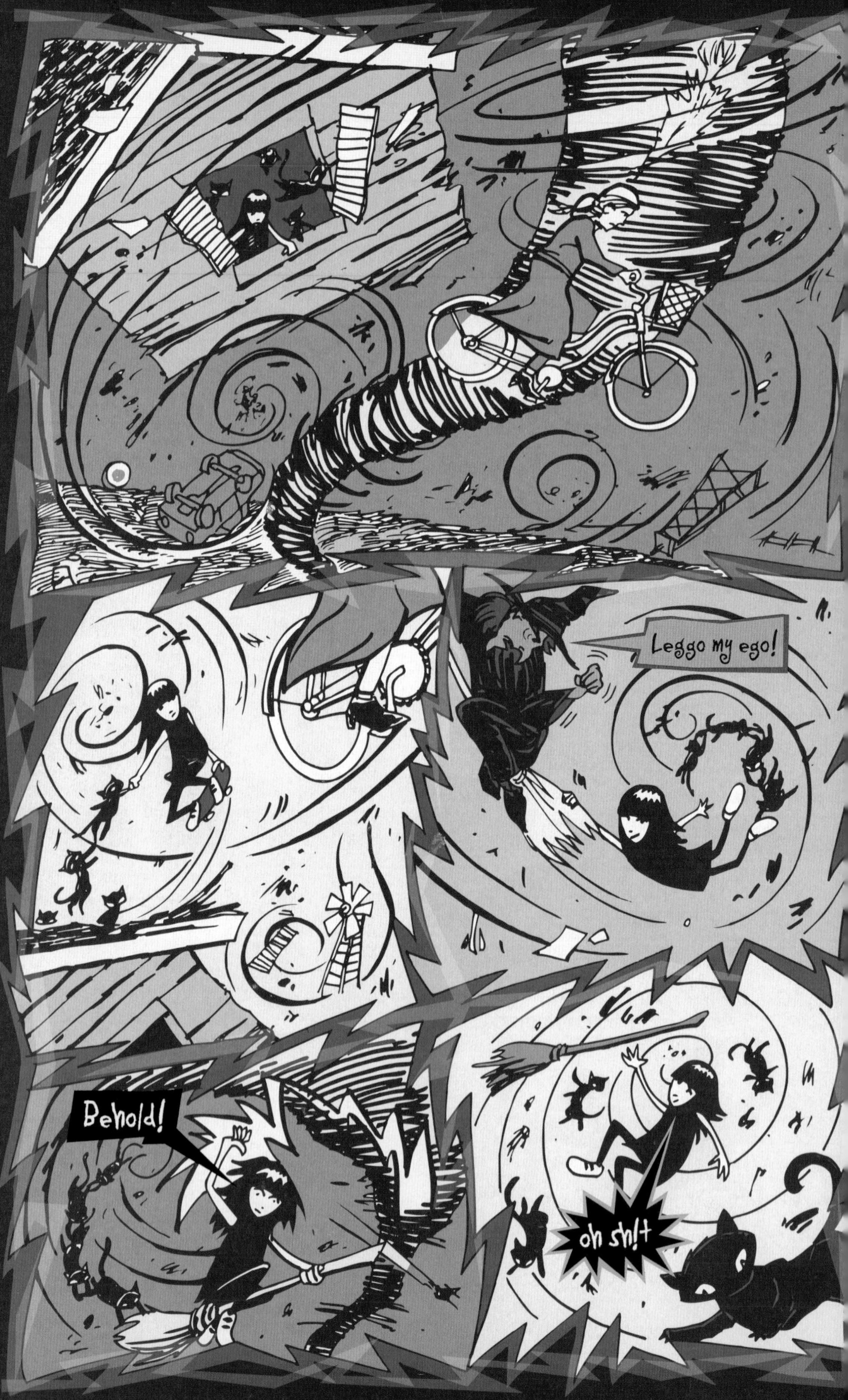
Leggo my ego!
Behold!
oh sh!t

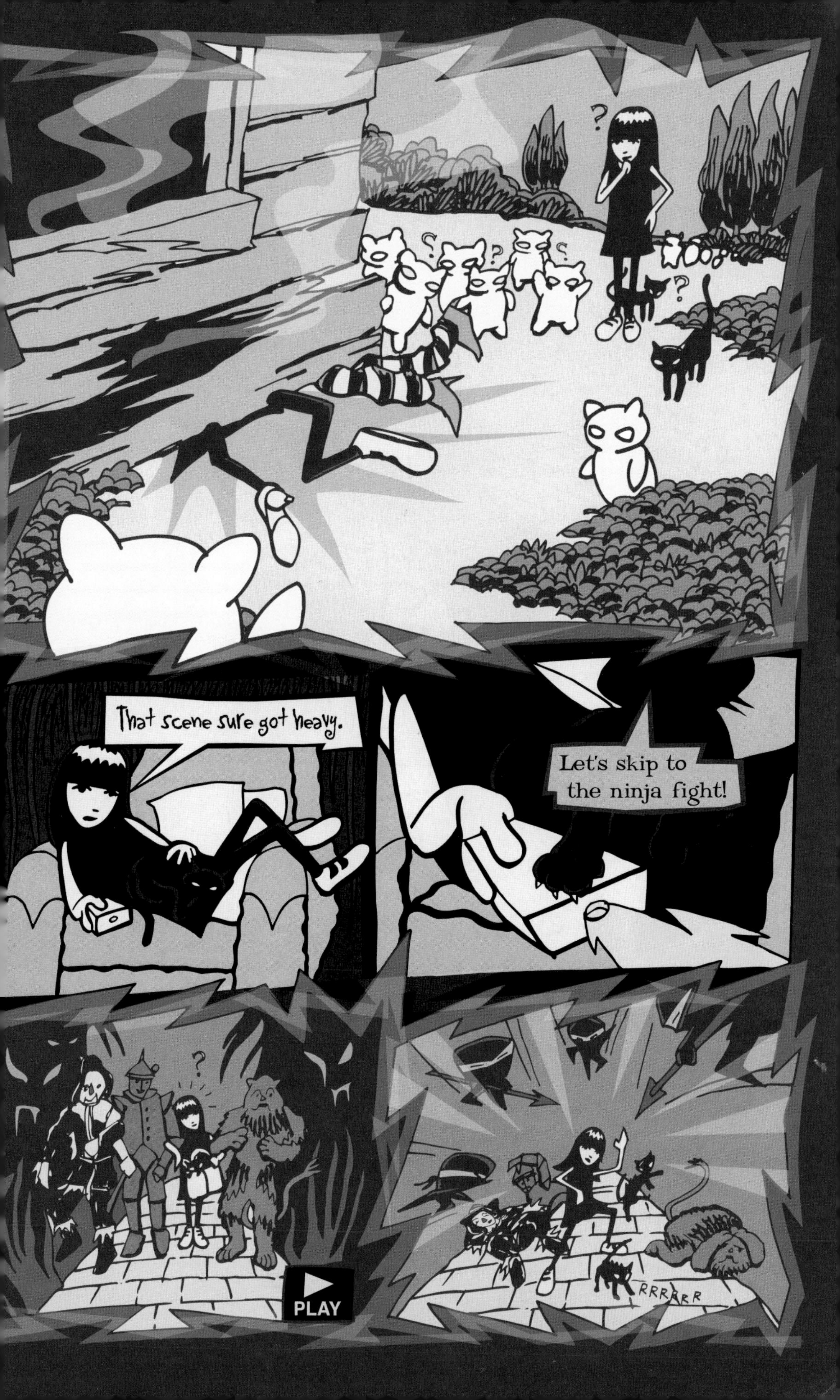

That scene sure got heavy.
Let's skip to the ninja fight!
PLAY
RRRRRR

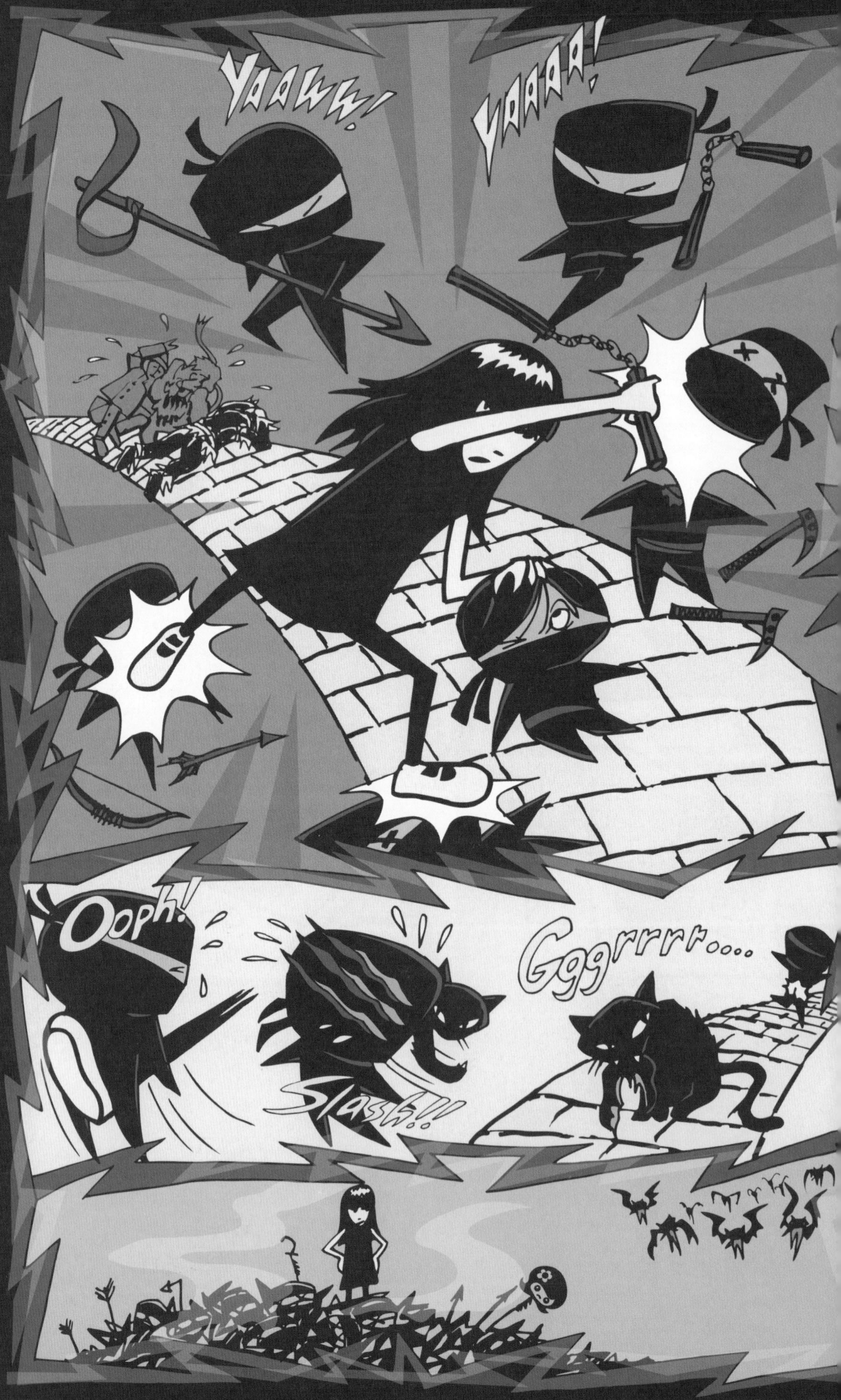

YAAWW!
YAAAA!
Ooph!
Slash!!
Gggrrrr....

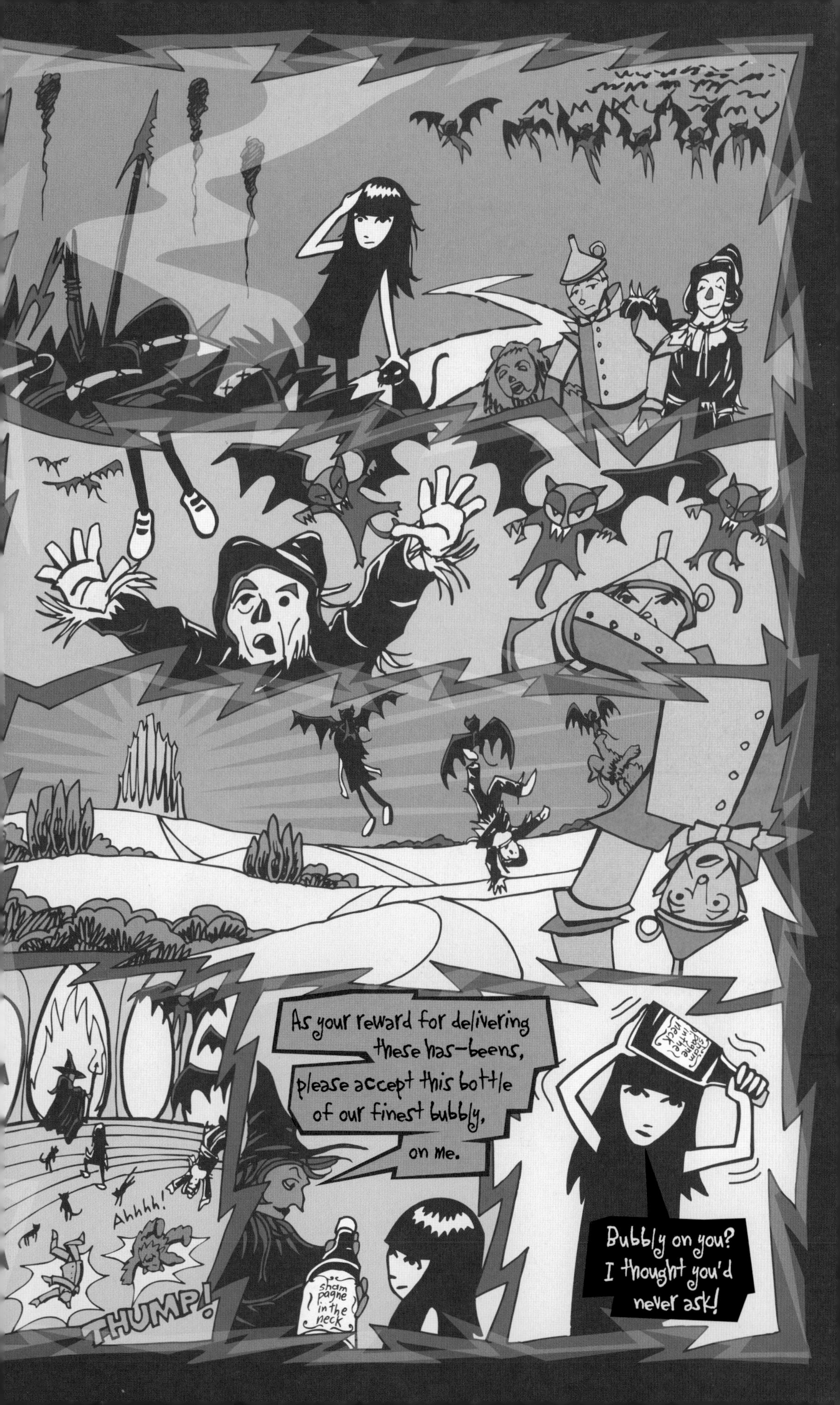

Ahhhh!
THUMP!
As your reward for delivering these has-beens, please accept this bottle of our finest bubbly, on me.
sham pagne in the neck
Bubbly on you? I thought you'd never ask!

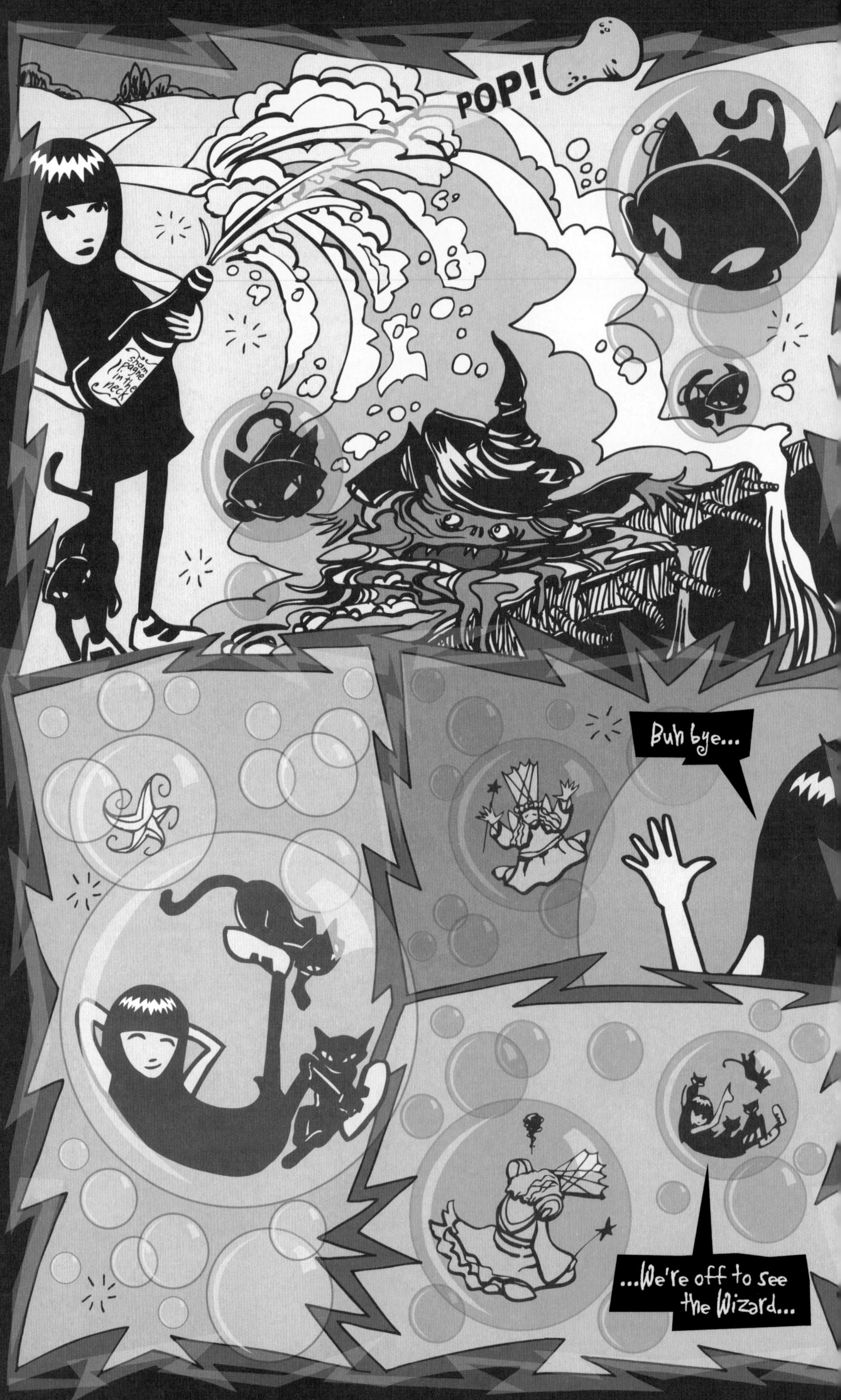
POP!
sham pagne in the neck
Buh bye...
...We're off to see the Wizard...

The Wonderful Blizzard of OZZ
I am Ozzy The Great and Terrible...
evil powers disappear
...and I can't find the f*©k!ng remote!
RUMBLE
SMASH!
You're no wizard...
...but you ARE The Prince of Darkness. You're also late for dinner.
Sharon
Oh sh...
There's no place like home.
everyone's happy when the Wizard goes by!
That's not the way the movie ends!
It is now!
CLICK!

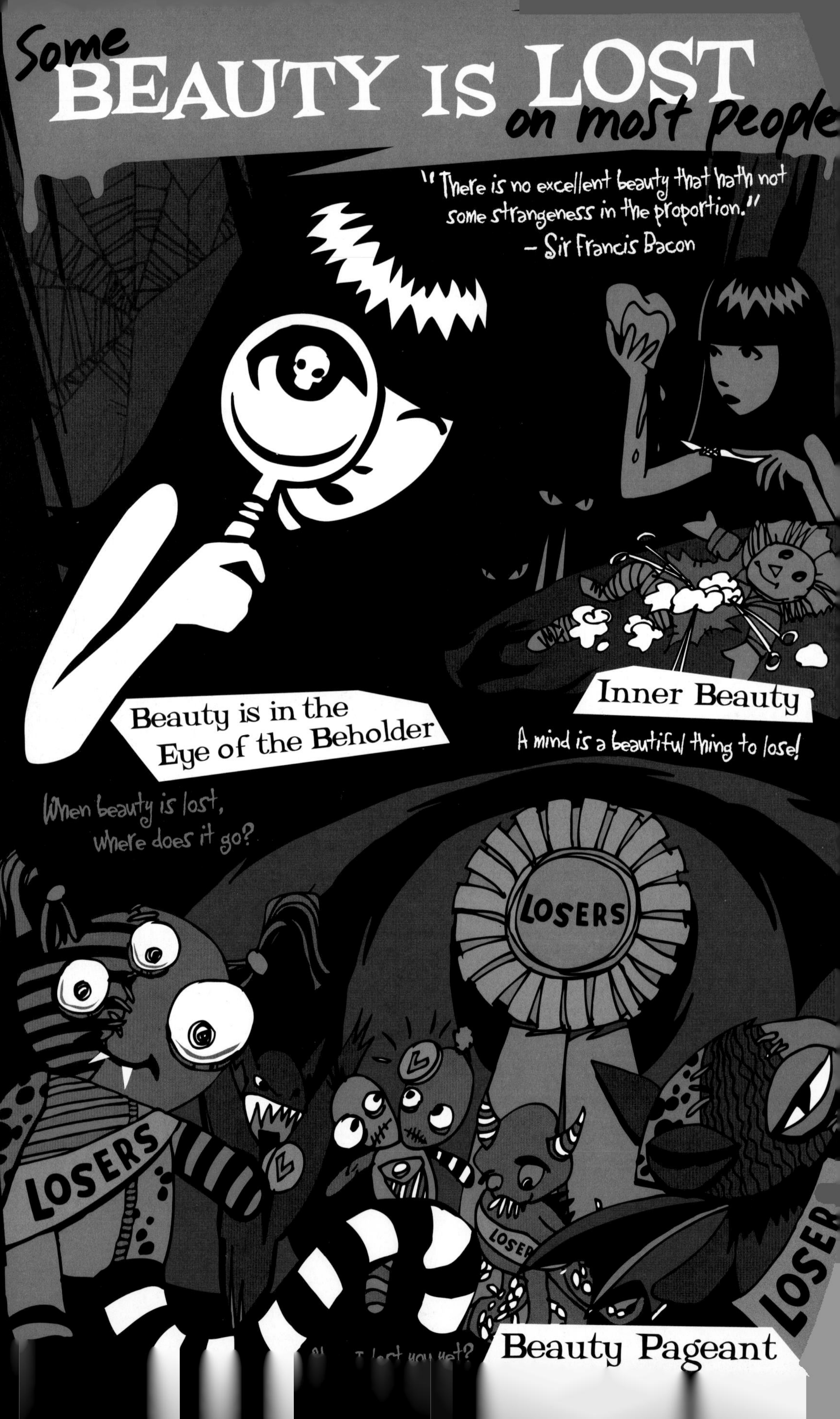

Some BEAUTY IS LOST on most people
"There is no excellent beauty that hath not some strangeness in the proportion."
– Sir Francis Bacon
Beauty is in the Eye of the Beholder
Inner Beauty
A mind is a beautiful thing to lose!
When beauty is lost, where does it go?
LOSERS
LOSERS
LOSER
LOSER
Beauty Pageant

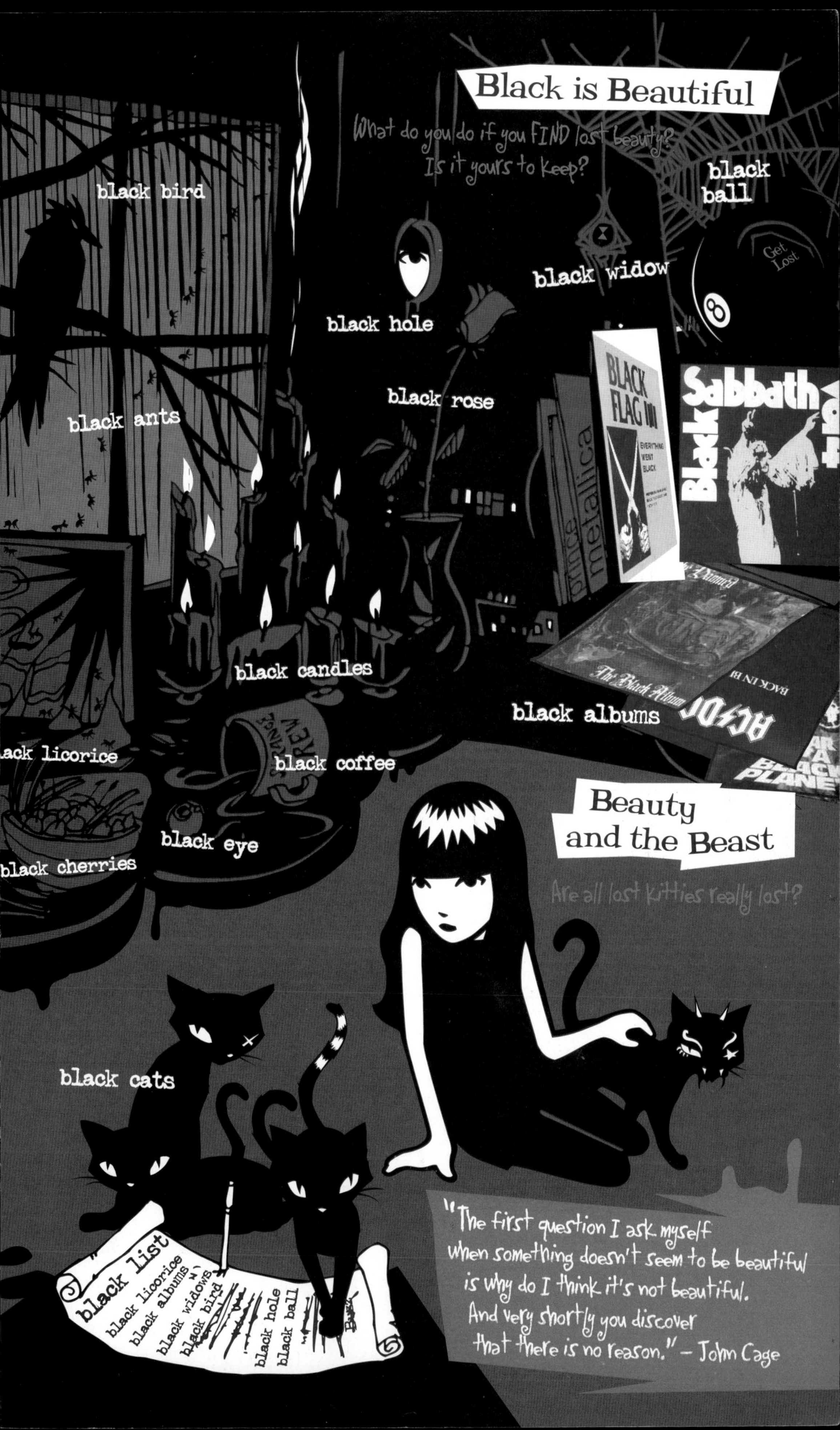
Black is Beautiful
What do you do if you FIND lost beauty?
Is it yours to keep?
black bird
black ball
Get Lost
black widow
black hole
black rose
BLACK FLAG
EVERYTHING WENT BLACK
Black Sabbath
prince
metallica
black ants
The Black Album
AC/DC
black candles
black albums
ack licorice
black coffee
Beauty and the Beast
black eye
black cherries
Are all lost kitties really lost?
black cats
black list
black licorice
black albums
black widows
black bird
black hole
black ball
"The first question I ask myself
when something doesn't seem to be beautiful
is why do I think it's not beautiful.
And very shortly you discover
that there is no reason." – John Cage

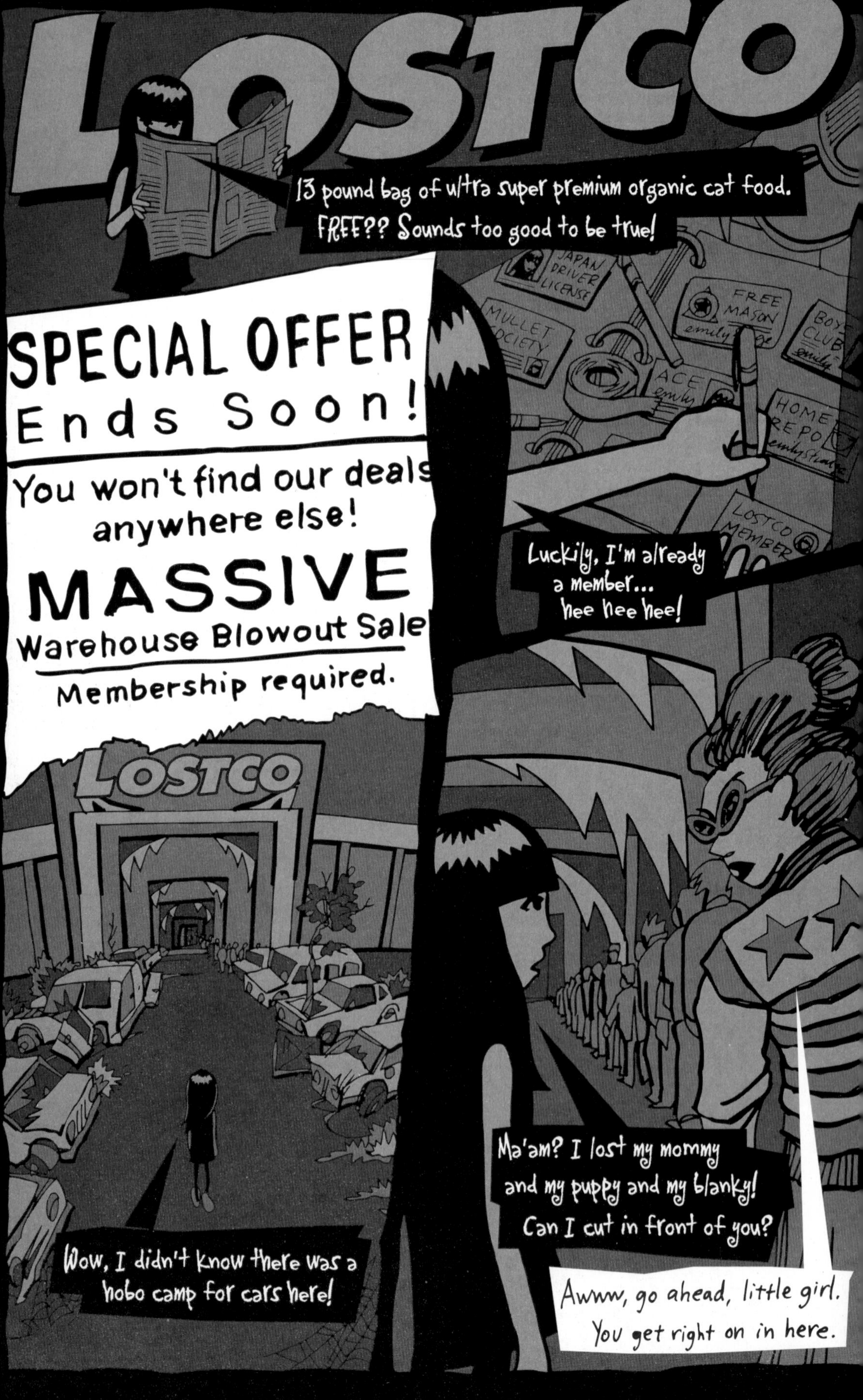
LOSTCO
13 pound bag of ultra super premium organic cat food. FREE?? Sounds too good to be true!
JAPAN DRIVER LICENSE
MULLET SOCIETY
FREE MASON
BOYS CLUB
ACE
HOME REPO
LOSTCO MEMBER
SPECIAL OFFER
Ends Soon!
You won't find our deals anywhere else!
MASSIVE
Warehouse Blowout Sale
Membership required.
Luckily, I'm already a member... hee hee hee!
LOSTCO
Wow, I didn't know there was a hobo camp for cars here!
Ma'am? I lost my mommy and my puppy and my blanky! Can I cut in front of you?
Awww, go ahead, little girl. You get right on in here.

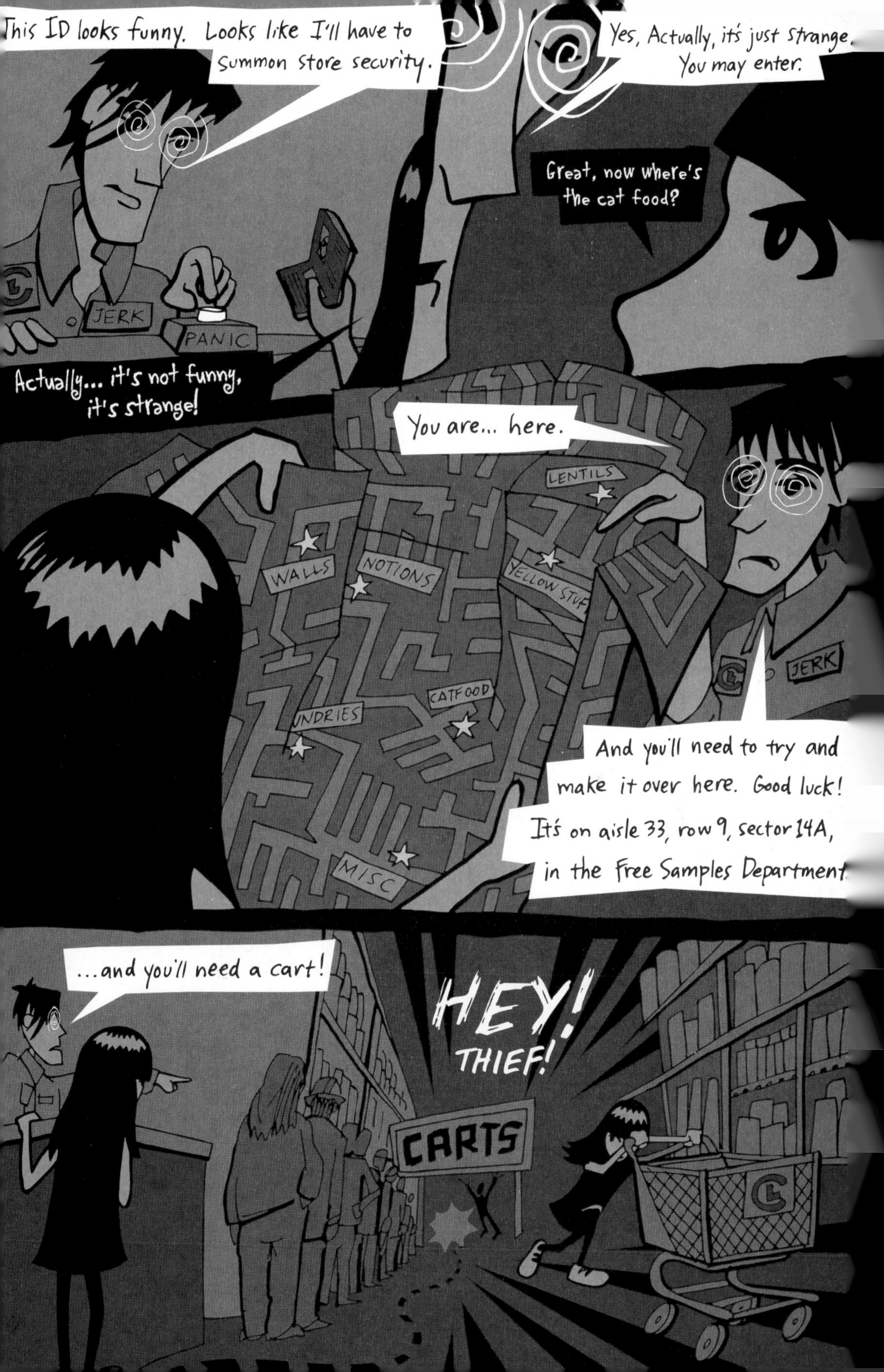
This ID looks funny. Looks like I'll have to summon store security.
Yes, Actually, it's just strange. You may enter.
Great, now where's the cat food?
JERK
PANIC
Actually... it's not funny, it's strange!
You are... here.
LENTILS
WALLS
NOTIONS
YELLOW STUF
CATFOOD
UNDRIES
MISC
JERK
And you'll need to try and make it over here. Good luck! It's on aisle 33, row 9, sector 14A, in the Free Samples Department.
...and you'll need a cart!
HEY!
THIEF!
CARTS

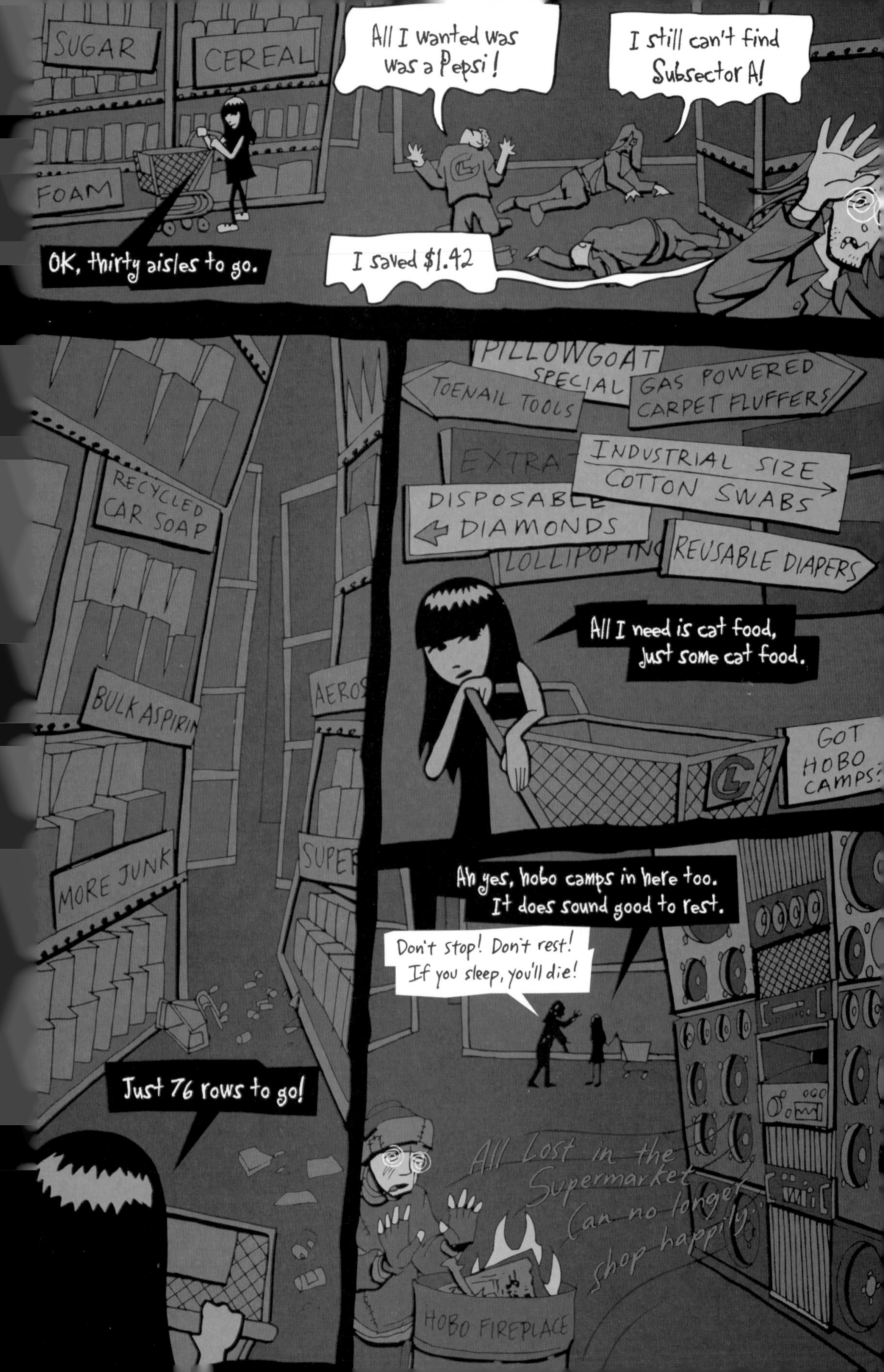
SUGAR
CEREAL
FOAM
OK, thirty aisles to go.
All I wanted was was a Pepsi!
I still can't find Subsector A!
I saved $1.42
PILLOWGOAT SPECIAL
TOENAIL TOOLS
GAS POWERED CARPET FLUFFERS
INDUSTRIAL SIZE COTTON SWABS
DISPOSABLE DIAMONDS
REUSABLE DIAPERS
RECYCLED CAR SOAP
BULK ASPIRIN
MORE JUNK
All I need is cat food, just some cat food.
GOT HOBO CAMPS?
Ah yes, hobo camps in here too. It does sound good to rest.
Don't stop! Don't rest! If you sleep, you'll die!
Just 76 rows to go!
All Lost in the Supermarket (can no longer shop happily)
HOBO FIREPLACE

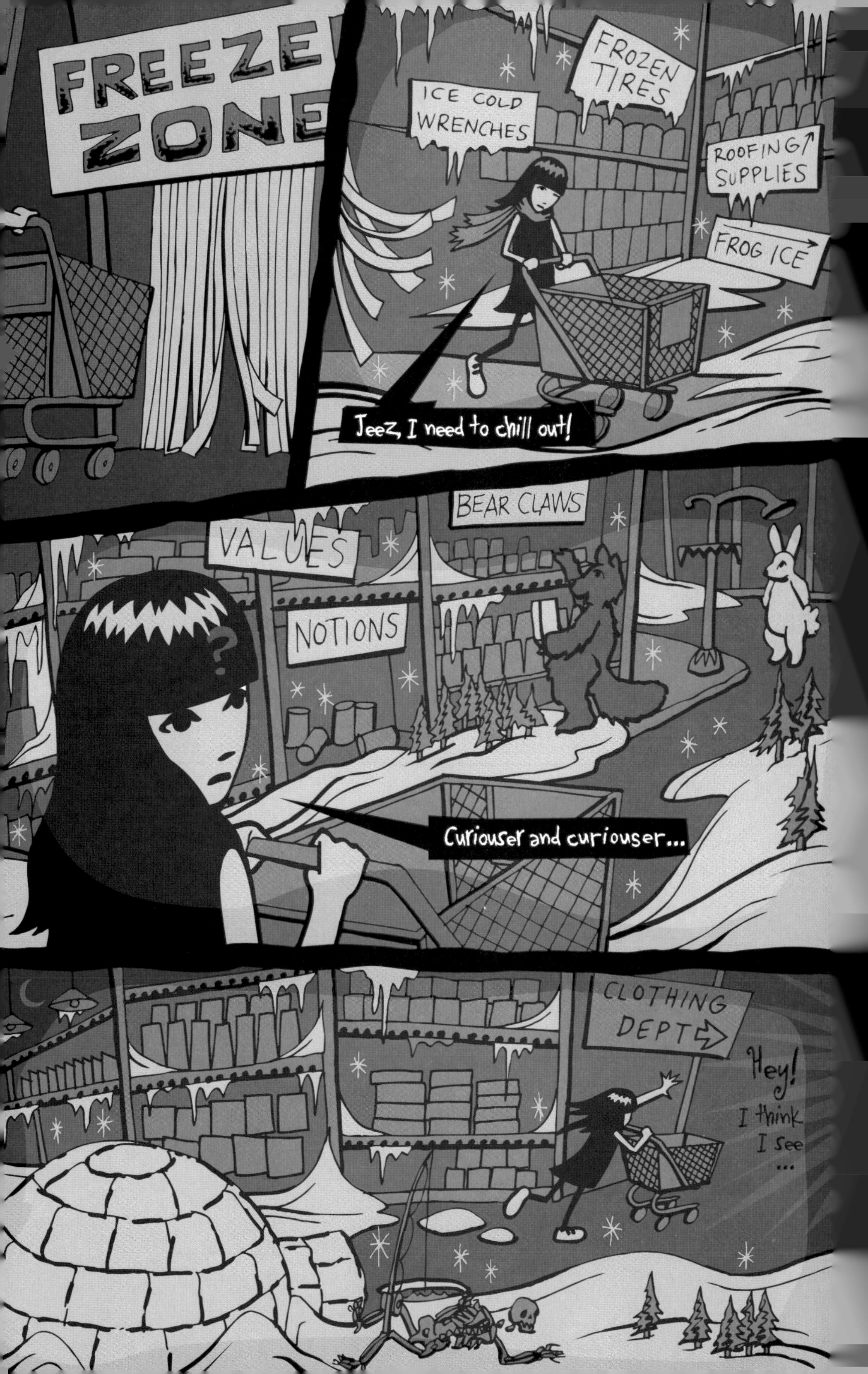
FREEZE ZONE
ICE COLD WRENCHES
FROZEN TIRES
ROOFING SUPPLIES
FROG ICE
Jeez, I need to chill out!
BEAR CLAWS
VALUES
NOTIONS
?
Curiouser and curiouser...
CLOTHING DEPT
Hey! I think I see ...

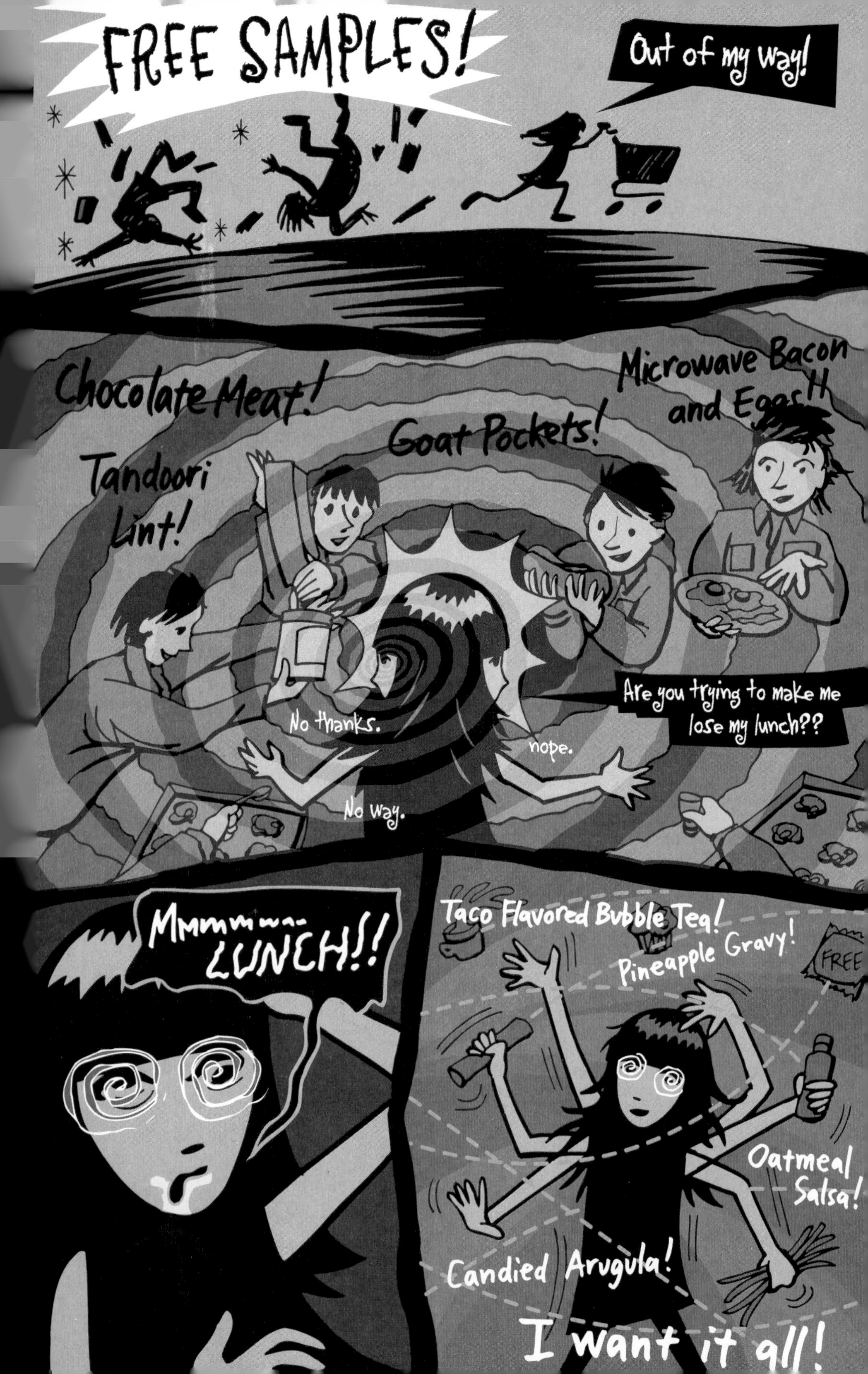

FREE SAMPLES!
Out of my way!
Chocolate Meat!
Microwave Bacon and Eggs!!
Goat Pockets!
Tandoori Lint!
Are you trying to make me lose my lunch??
No thanks.
nope.
No way.
Mmmmwa-- LUNCH!!
Taco Flavored Bubble Tea!
Pineapple Gravy!
FREE
Oatmeal Salsa!
Candied Arugula!
I want it all!

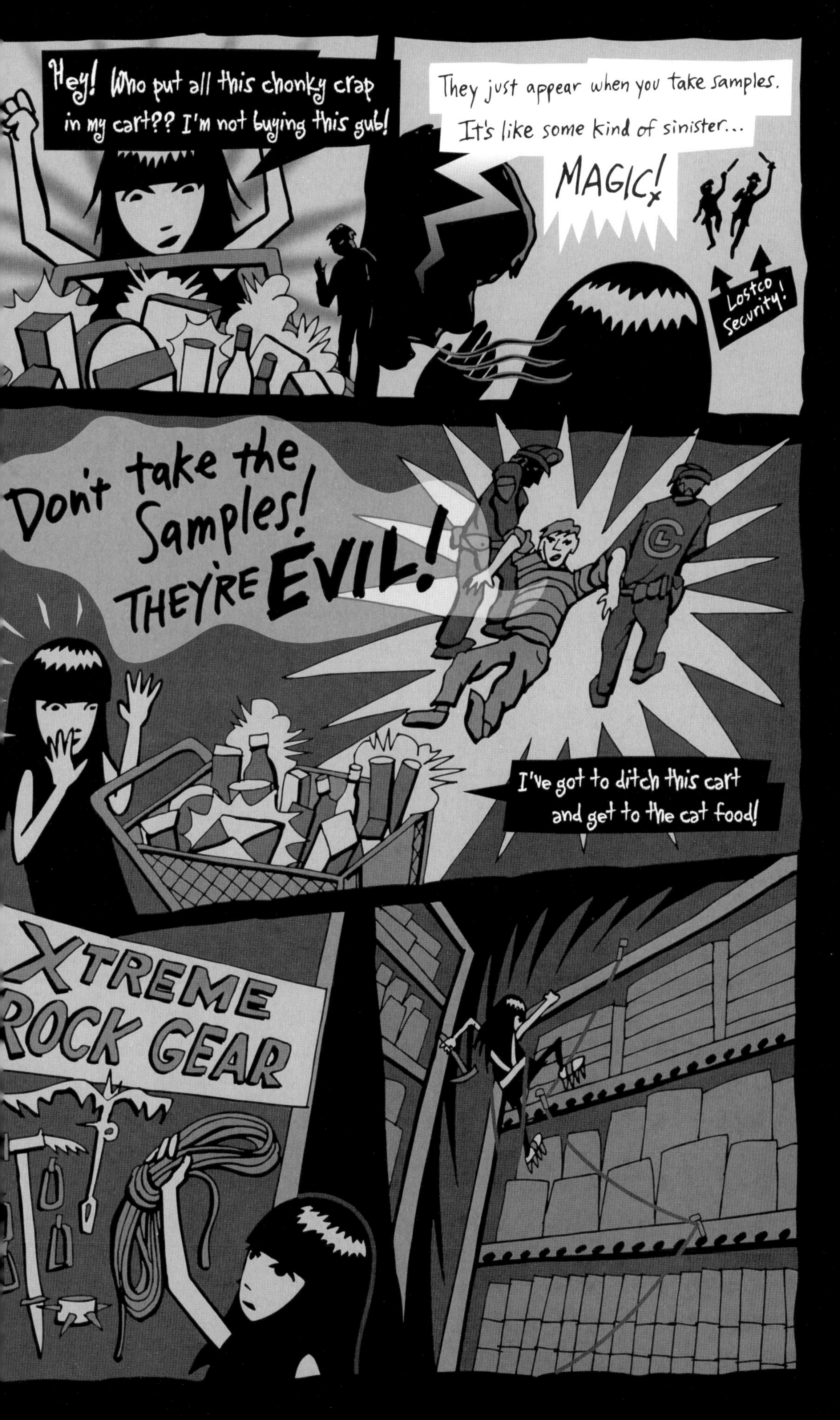
Hey! Who put all this chonky crap in my cart?? I'm not buying this gub!
They just appear when you take samples. It's like some kind of sinister...
MAGIC!
Lostco Security!
Don't take the Samples! THEY'RE EVIL!
I've got to ditch this cart and get to the cat food!
XTREME ROCK GEAR

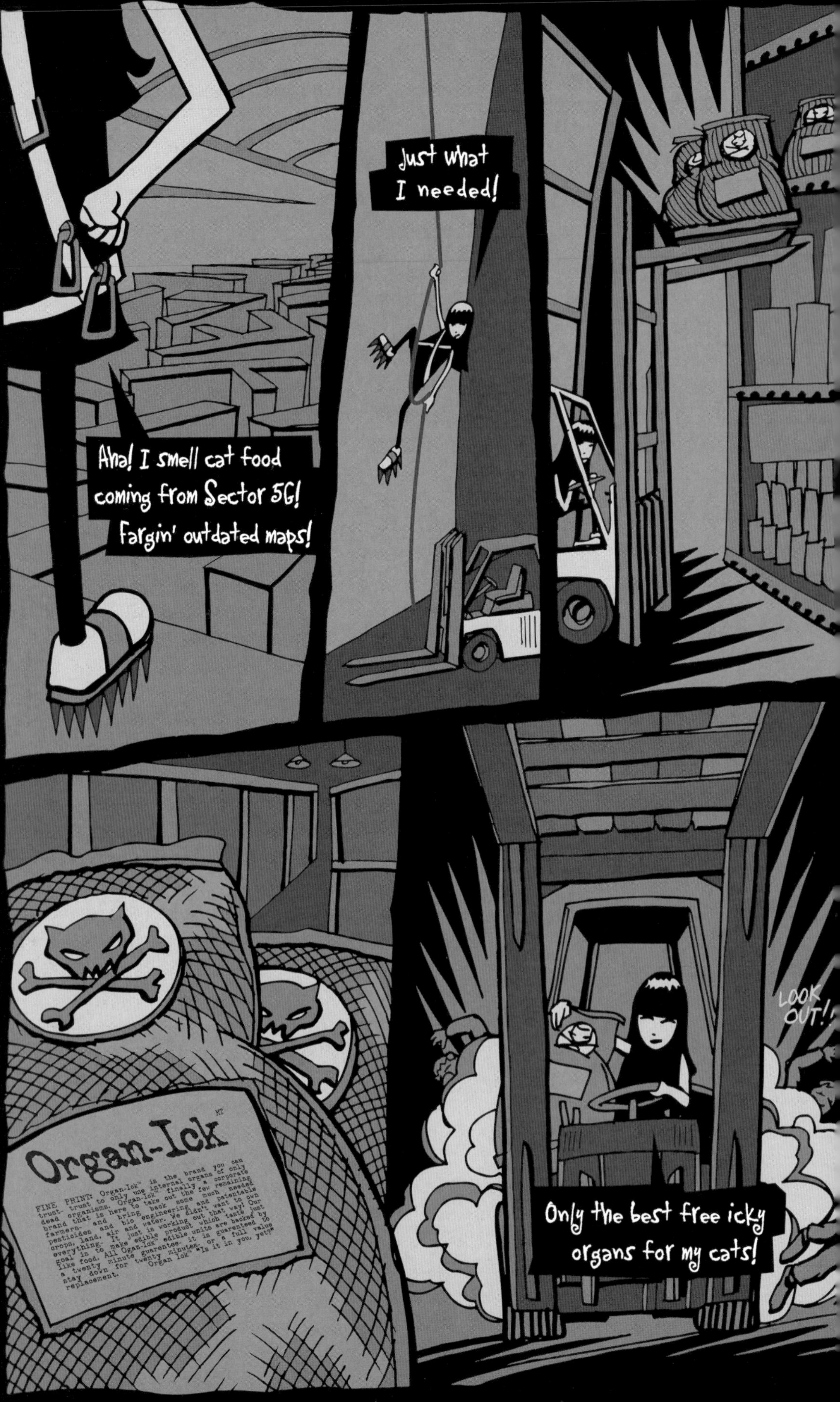

Aha! I smell cat food coming from Sector 5G! Fargin' outdated maps!
Just what I needed!
Organ-Ick MT
FINE PRINT: Organ-Ick™ is the brand you can trust- trust to only use internal organs of only dead organisms. Organ-Ick™ finally a corporate brand that is here to take out the few remaining farmers- and bring back some much needed pesticides and bio engineering and patentable crops, land, air and water. We didn't want to own everything- It just is working out that way! Our goal is to make edible product which taste just like food. All Ogan-Ick™ edible units are backed by a twenty minute guarentee- it is guarenteed to stay down for twenty minutes- or a full value replacement. Organ Ick™ "Is it in you, yet?"
LOOK OUT!!
Only the best free icky organs for my cats!

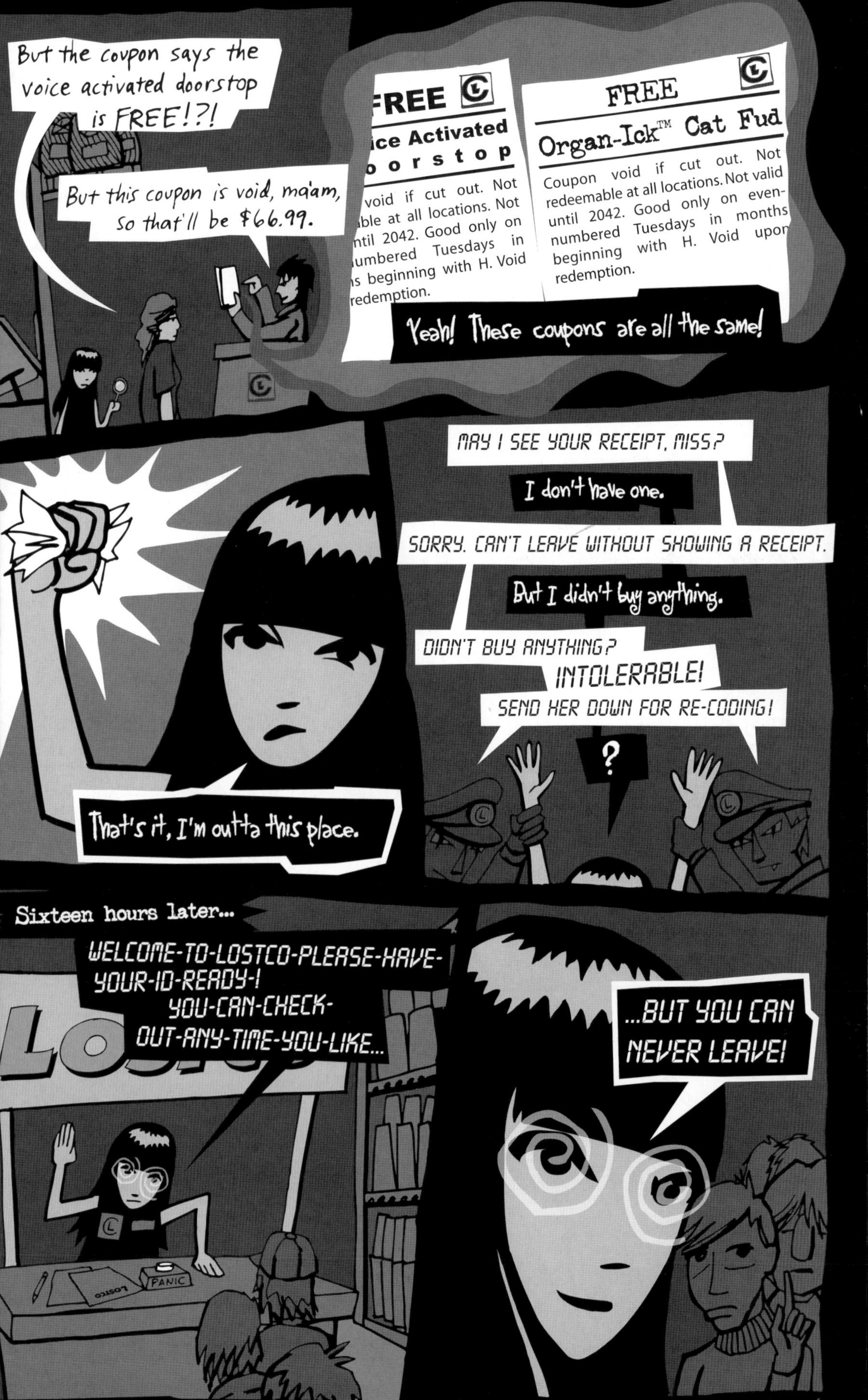
But the coupon says the voice activated doorstop is FREE!?!
But this coupon is void, ma'am, so that'll be $66.99.
FREE
ice Activated
oorstop
void if cut out. Not
ble at all locations. Not
ntil 2042. Good only on
umbered Tuesdays in
s beginning with H. Void
redemption.
FREE
Organ-Ick™ Cat Fud
Coupon void if cut out. Not redeemable at all locations. Not valid until 2042. Good only on even-numbered Tuesdays in months beginning with H. Void upon redemption.
Yeah! These coupons are all the same!
That's it, I'm outta this place.
MAY I SEE YOUR RECEIPT, MISS?
I don't have one.
SORRY. CAN'T LEAVE WITHOUT SHOWING A RECEIPT.
But I didn't buy anything.
DIDN'T BUY ANYTHING?
INTOLERABLE!
SEND HER DOWN FOR RE-CODING!
?
Sixteen hours later...
WELCOME-TO-LOSTCO-PLEASE-HAVE-YOUR-ID-READY-!
YOU-CAN-CHECK-OUT-ANY-TIME-YOU-LIKE...
...BUT YOU CAN NEVER LEAVE!
PANIC

Lost City
Lost keys stay lost.
Lost goat, sorry, no room in the attic for you.
Lost marbles, got enough.
Nothing like chewing gum on a string for finding lost treasures!
N
W
S
E
Wicked! Someone lost their treasure map!
This could be the find of a lifetime... The Lost City!

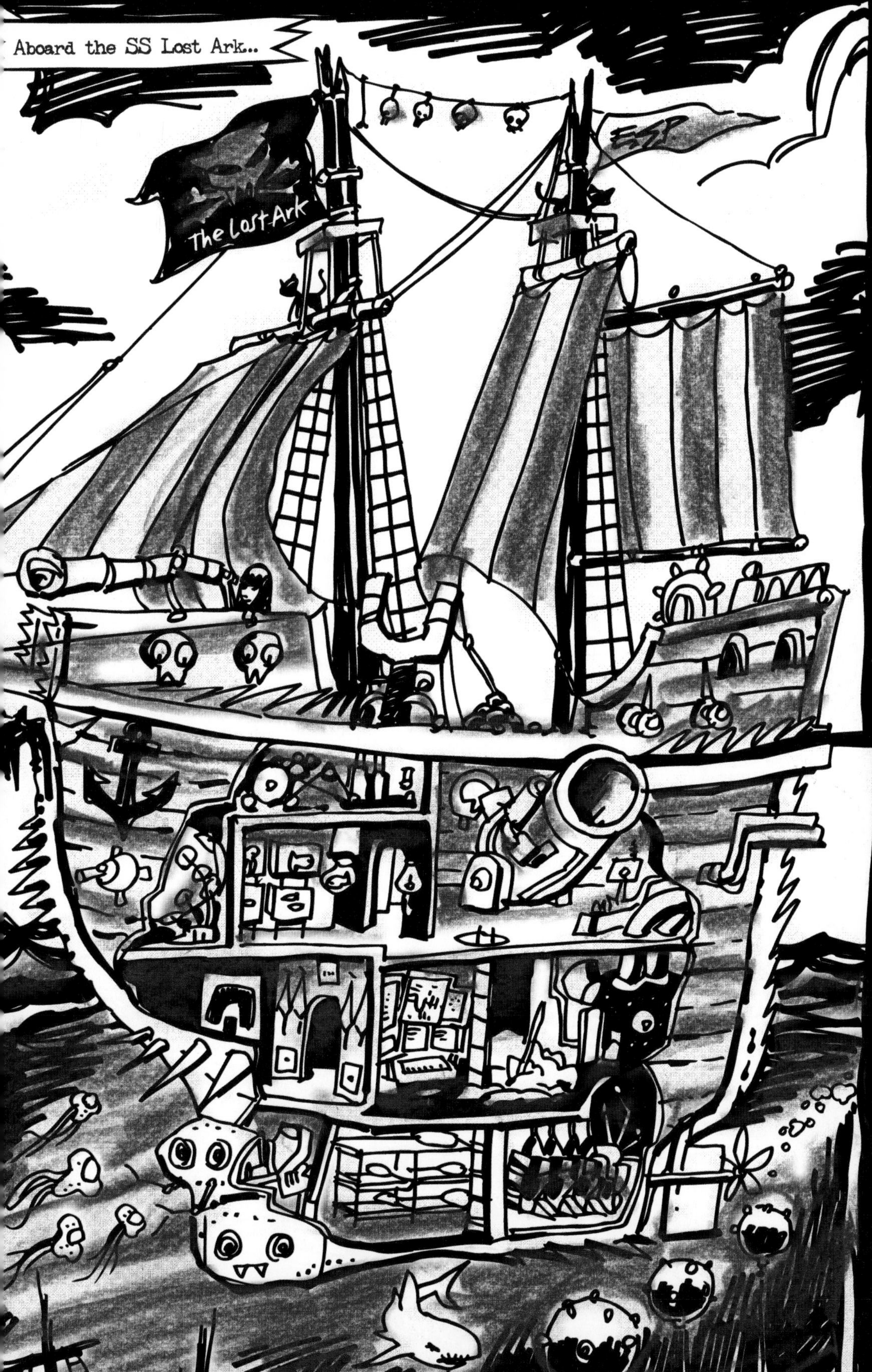

Aboard the SS Lost Ark..
The Lost Ark
ESP

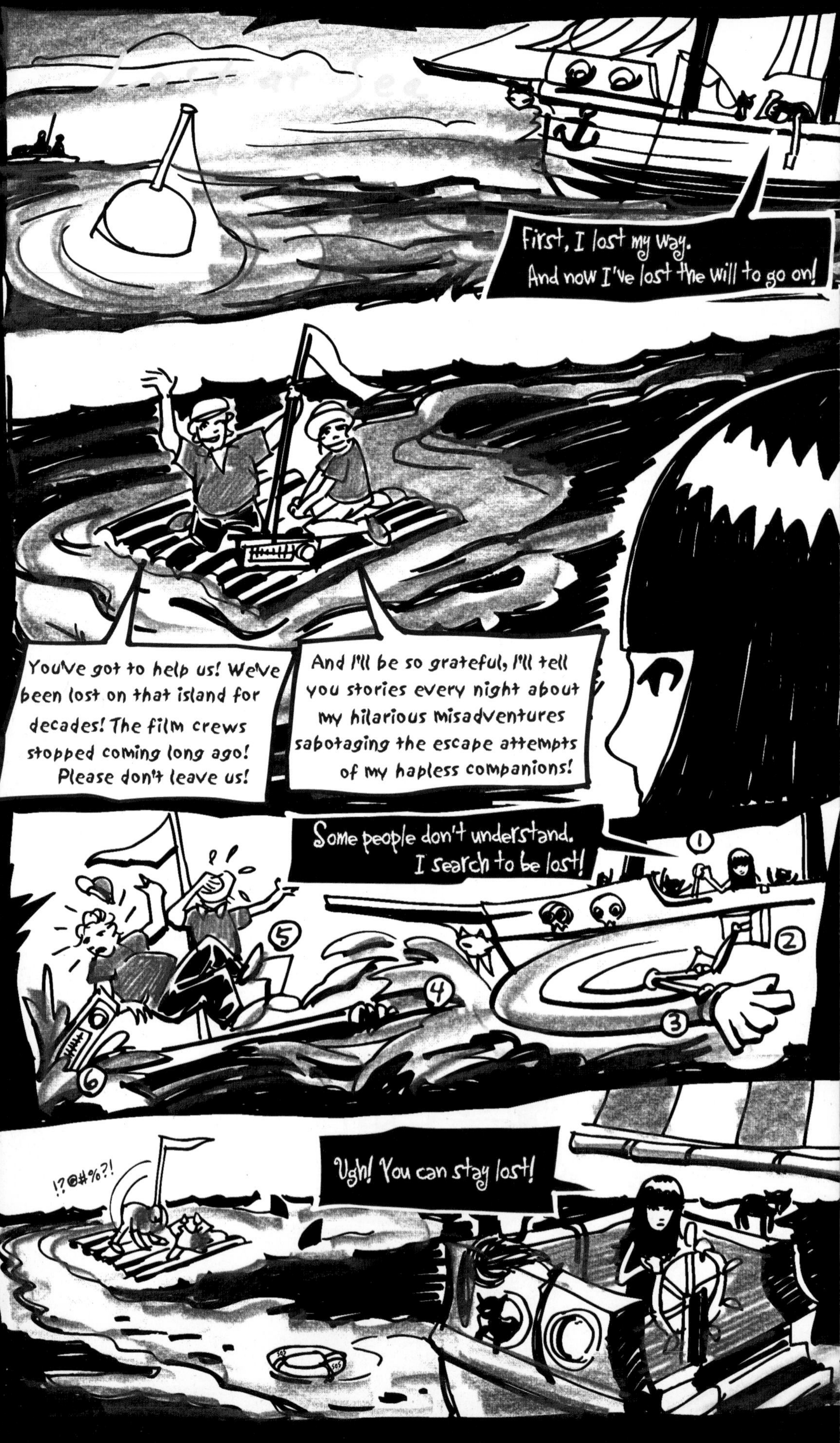

Lost at Sea
First, I lost my way.
And now I've lost the will to go on!
You've got to help us! We've been lost on that island for decades! The film crews stopped coming long ago! Please don't leave us!
And I'll be so grateful, I'll tell you stories every night about my hilarious misadventures sabotaging the escape attempts of my hapless companions!
Some people don't understand. I search to be lost!
1
2
3
4
5
6
!?@#%?!
Ugh! You can stay lost!

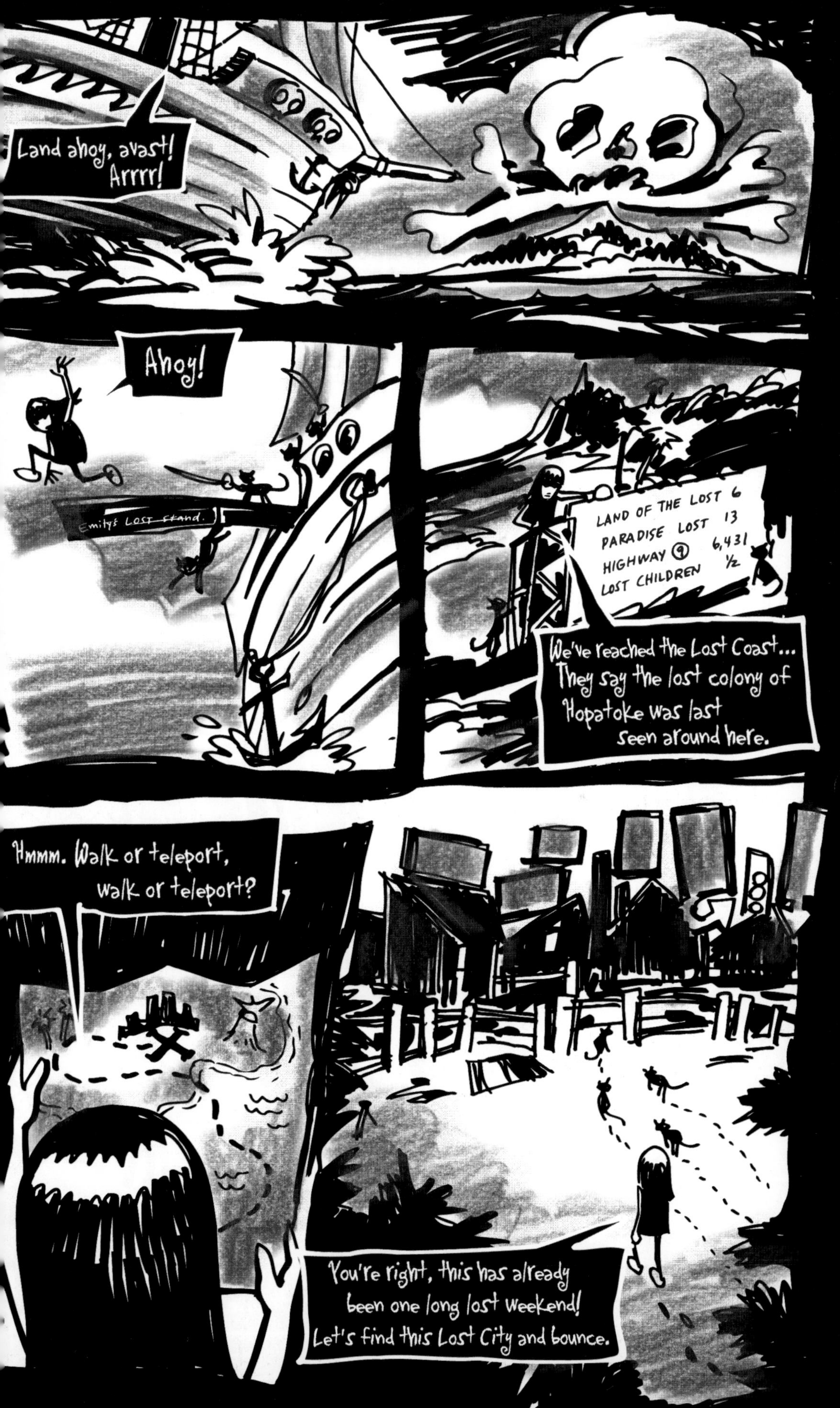
Land ahoy, avast! Arrrr!
Ahoy!
Emily's LOST stand.
LAND OF THE LOST 6
PARADISE LOST 13
HIGHWAY 9 6,431
LOST CHILDREN 1/2
We've reached the Lost Coast... They say the lost colony of Hopatoke was last seen around here.
Hmmm. Walk or teleport, walk or teleport?
You're right, this has already been one long lost weekend! Let's find this Lost City and bounce.

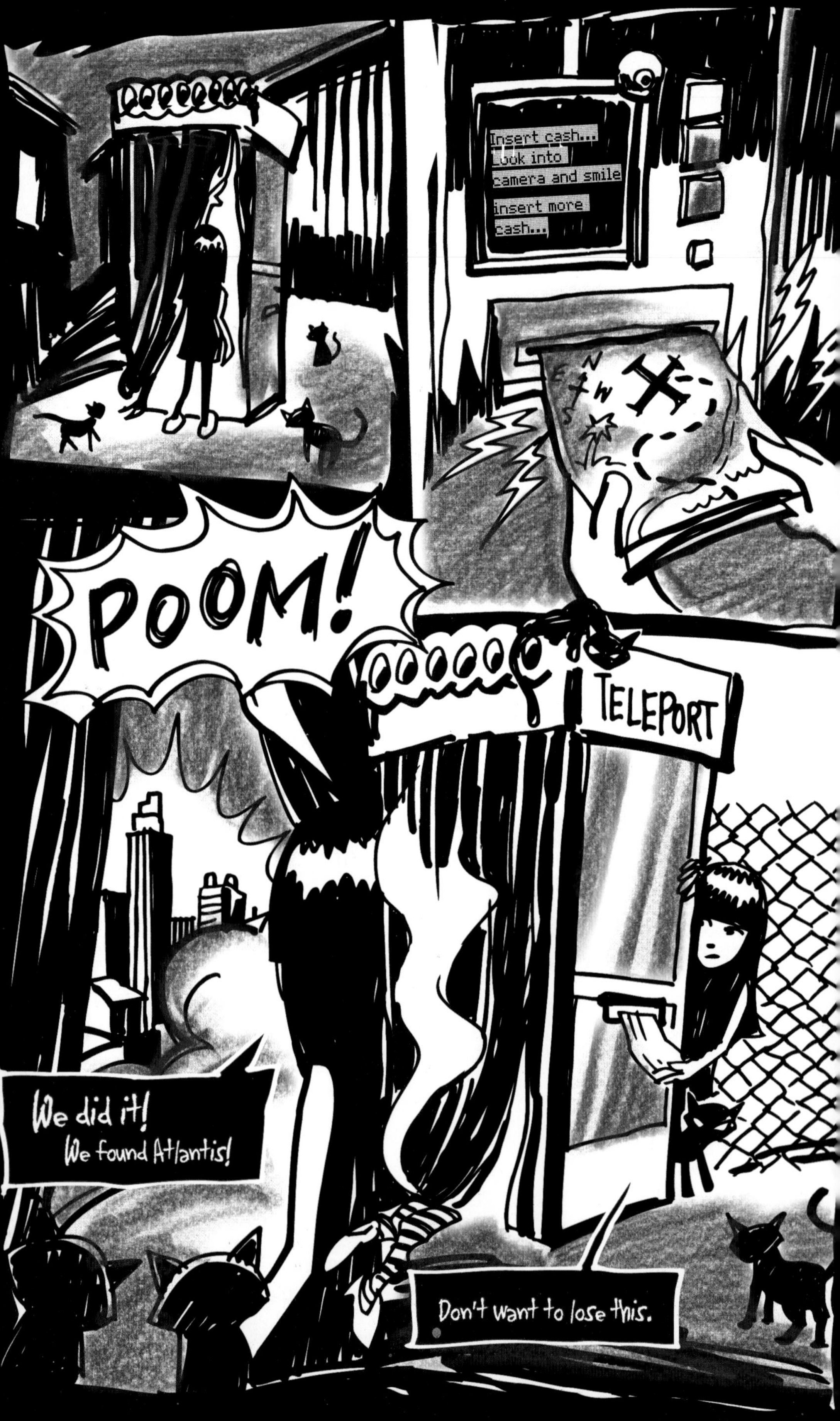
Insert cash...
Look into
camera and smile
insert more
cash...
N
E
W
S
POOM!
TELEPORT
We did it!
We found Atlantis!
Don't want to lose this.

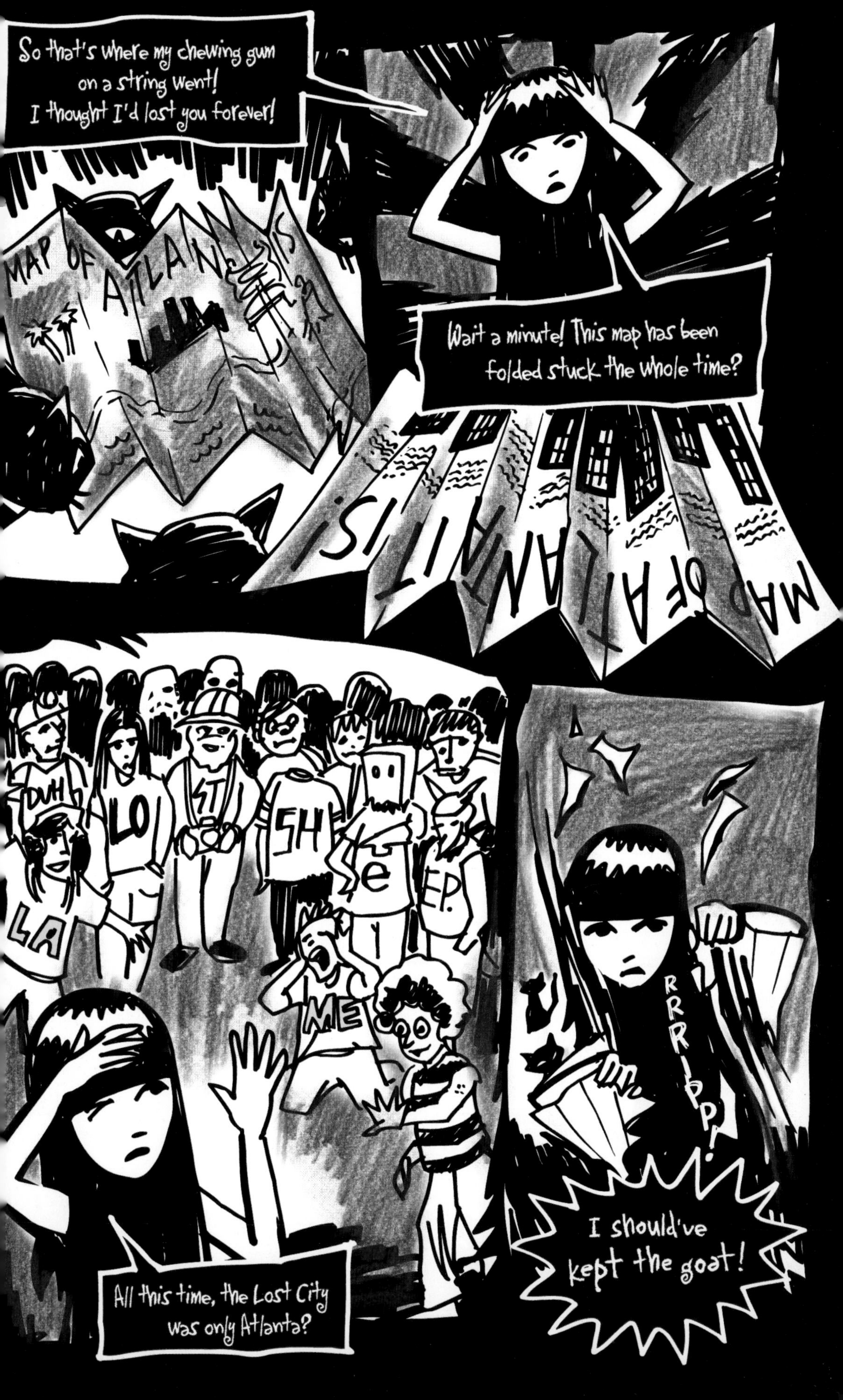
So that's where my chewing gum on a string went! I thought I'd lost you forever!
MAP OF ATLAN
IS
Wait a minute! This map has been folded stuck the whole time?
MAP OF ATLANTIS!
DUH
LO
ST
SH
e
EP.
LA
ME
All this time, the Lost City was only Atlanta?
RRRIPP!
I should've kept the goat!

LOST IN SPACE
LOST SCENES FROM LOST IN SPACE
Cool, Just one more Lost scene to write...
Oh no!
Strange brew on the Oddisee!
I'll lose my story!
HISSSSSS
ZOT!
ZZZZZZ

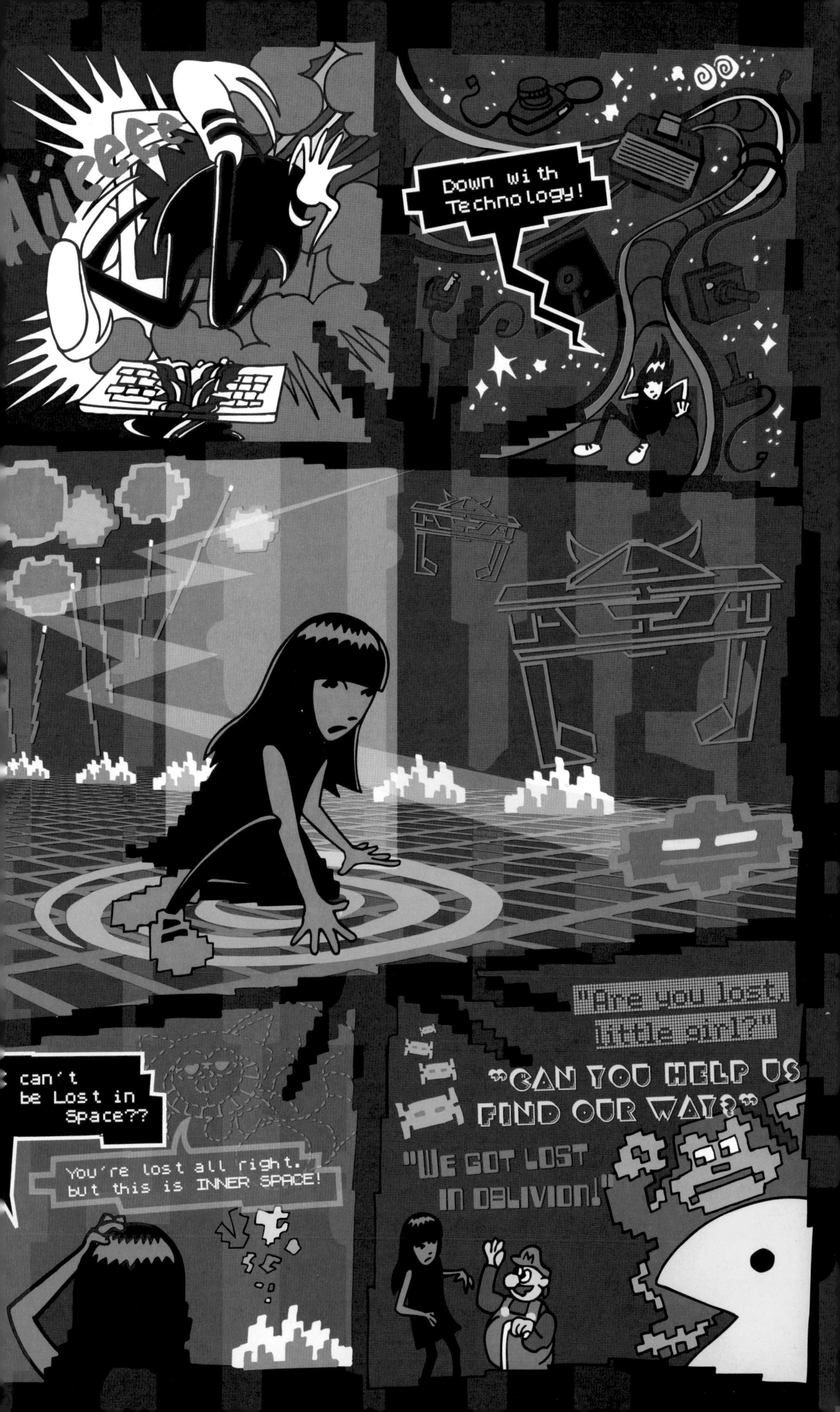
Aiieeee
Down with Technology!
can't be Lost in Space??
You're lost all right. but this is INNER SPACE!
"Are you lost, little girl?"
"CAN YOU HELP US FIND OUR WAY?"
"WE GOT LOST IN OBLIVION!"

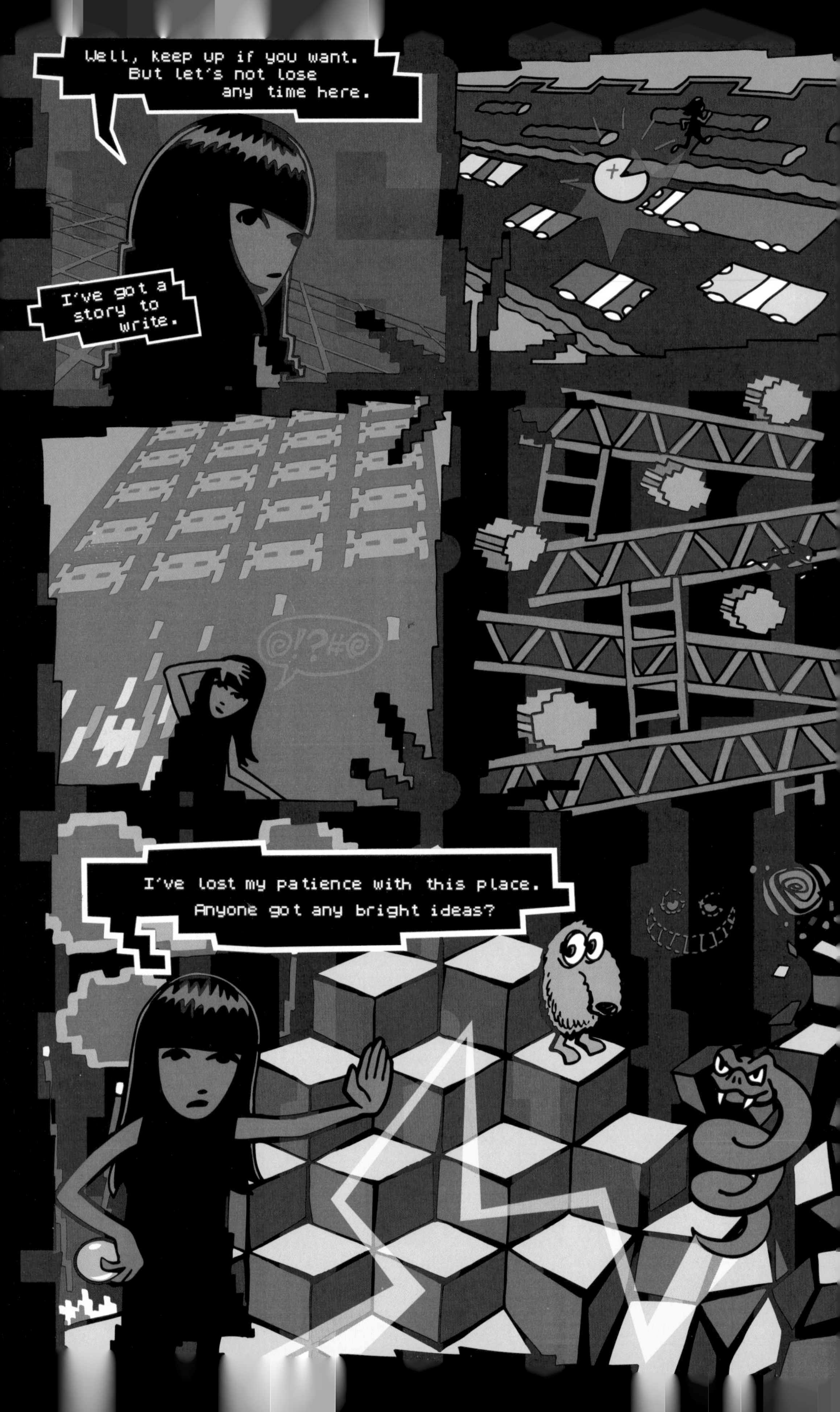
Well, keep up if you want. But let's not lose any time here.
I've got a story to write.
@!?#@
I've lost my patience with this place. Anyone got any bright ideas?

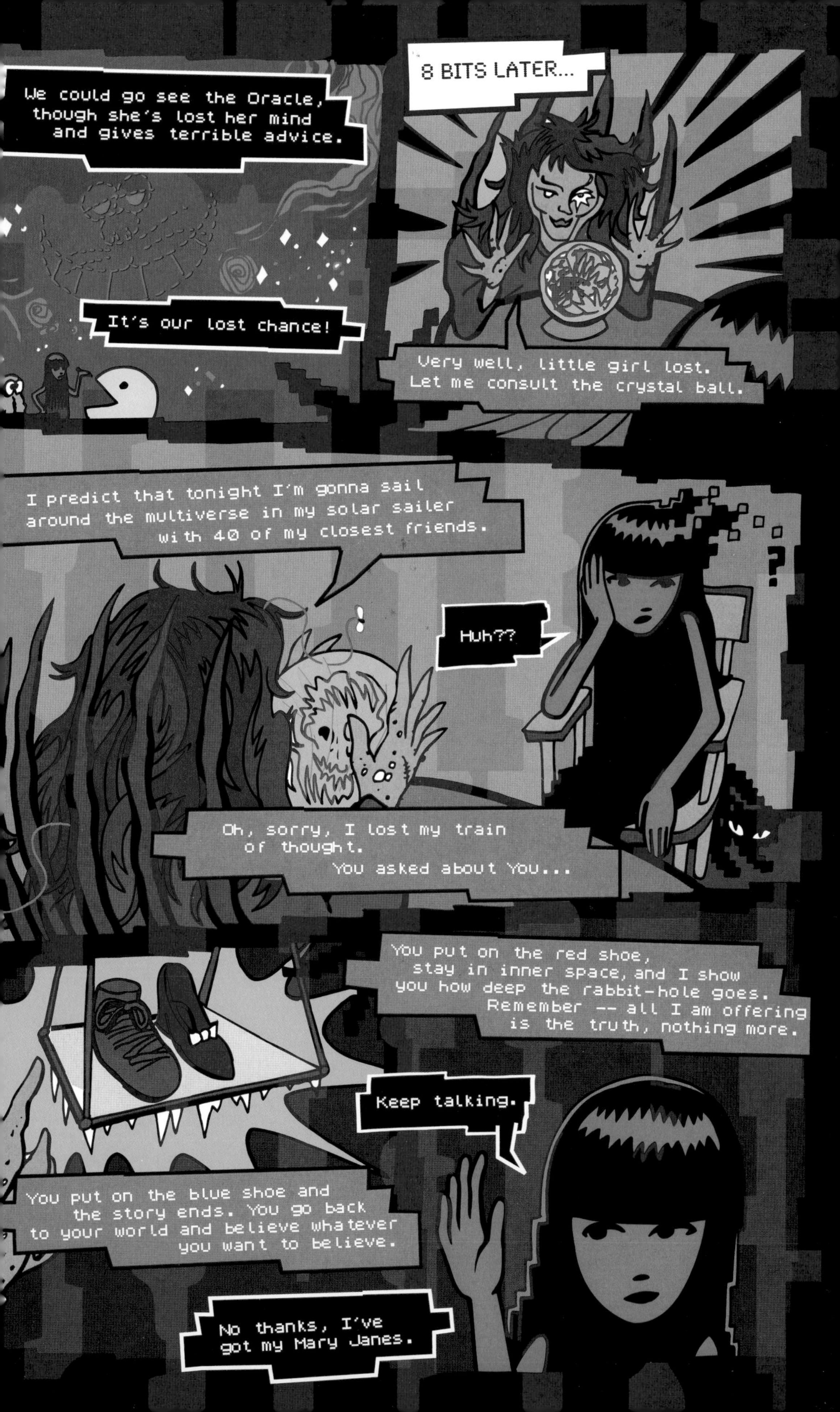

We could go see the Oracle, though she's lost her mind and gives terrible advice.
It's our lost chance!
8 BITS LATER...
Very well, little girl lost. Let me consult the crystal ball.
I predict that tonight I'm gonna sail around the multiverse in my solar sailer with 40 of my closest friends.
Huh??
Oh, sorry, I lost my train of thought. You asked about You...
You put on the red shoe, stay in inner space, and I show you how deep the rabbit-hole goes. Remember -- all I am offering is the truth, nothing more.
Keep talking.
You put on the blue shoe and the story ends. You go back to your world and believe whatever you want to believe.
No thanks, I've got my Mary Janes.

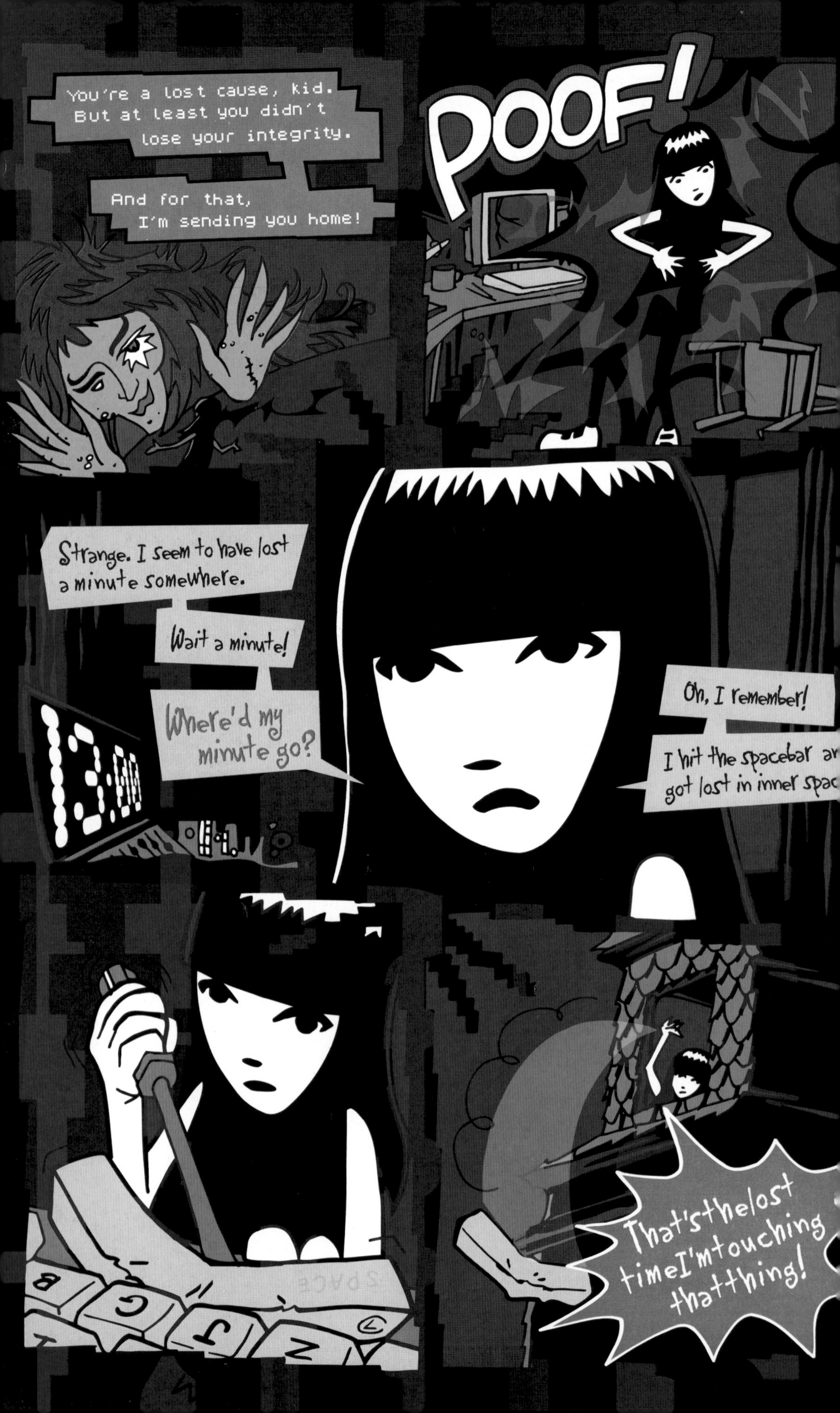
You're a lost cause, kid. But at least you didn't lose your integrity.
And for that, I'm sending you home!
POOF!
Strange. I seem to have lost a minute somewhere.
Wait a minute!
Where'd my minute go?
13:00
Oh, I remember!
I hit the spacebar
got lost in inner
SPACE
That's the lost time I'm touching that thing!

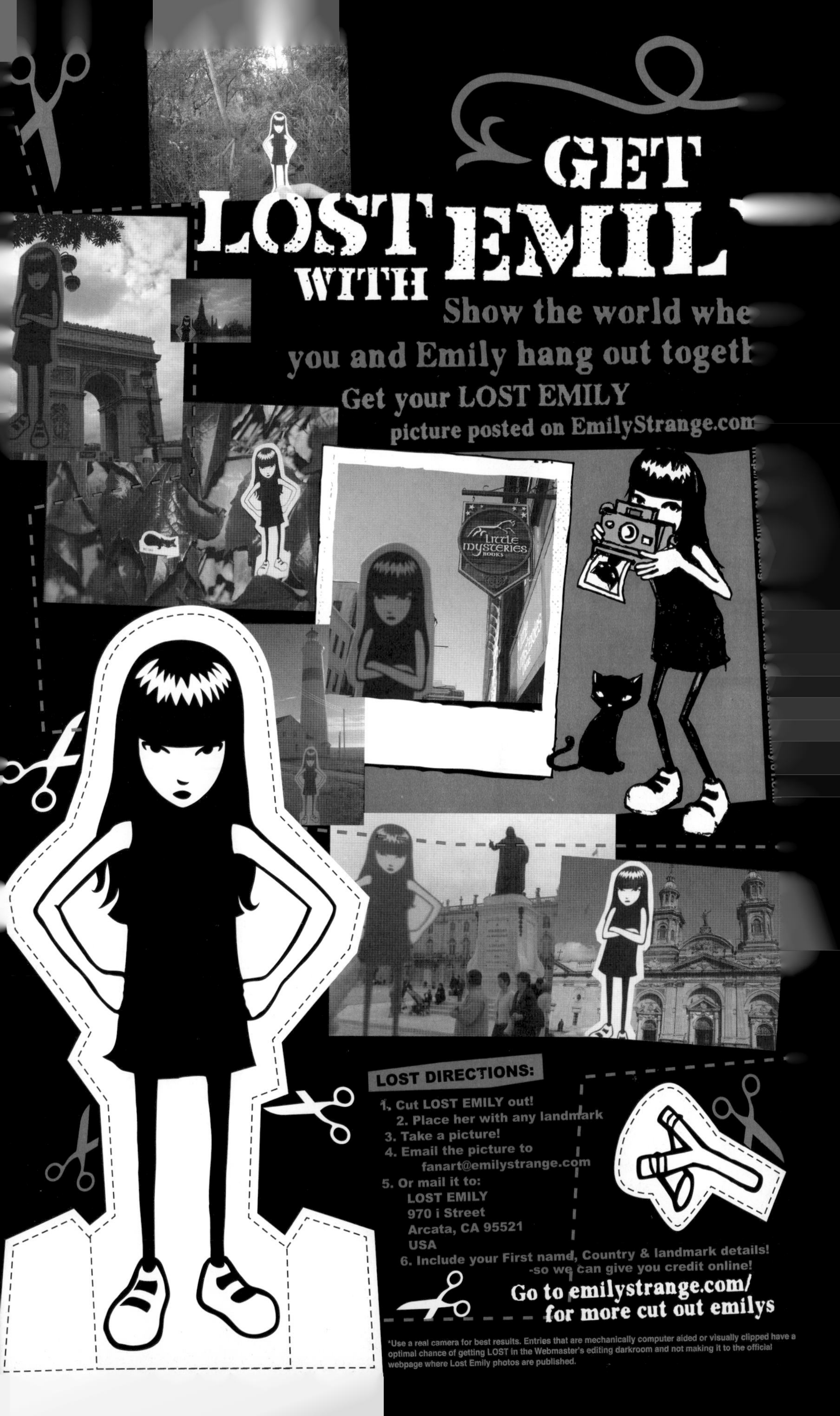

GET LOST WITH EMIL
Show the world whe
you and Emily hang out togetl
Get your LOST EMILY
picture posted on EmilyStrange.com
Little Mysteries Books
LOST DIRECTIONS:
1. Cut LOST EMILY out!
2. Place her with any landmark
3. Take a picture!
4. Email the picture to fanart@emilystrange.com
5. Or mail it to:
LOST EMILY
970 i Street
Arcata, CA 95521
USA
6. Include your First name, Country & landmark details!
-so we can give you credit online!
Go to emilystrange.com/
for more cut out emilys
*Use a real camera for best results. Entries that are mechanically computer aided or visually clipped have a optimal chance of getting LOST in the Webmaster's editing darkroom and not making it to the official webpage where Lost Emily photos are published.

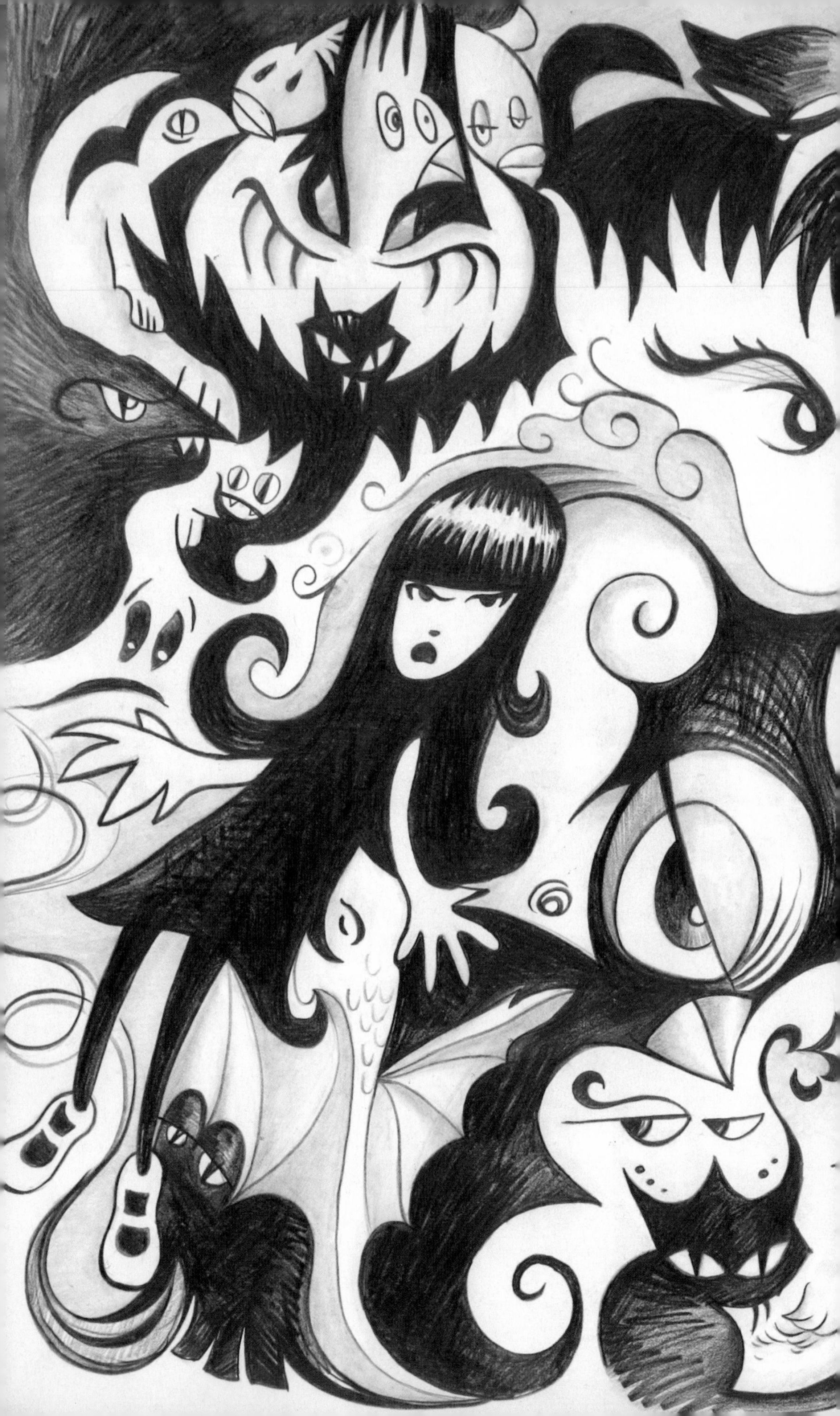

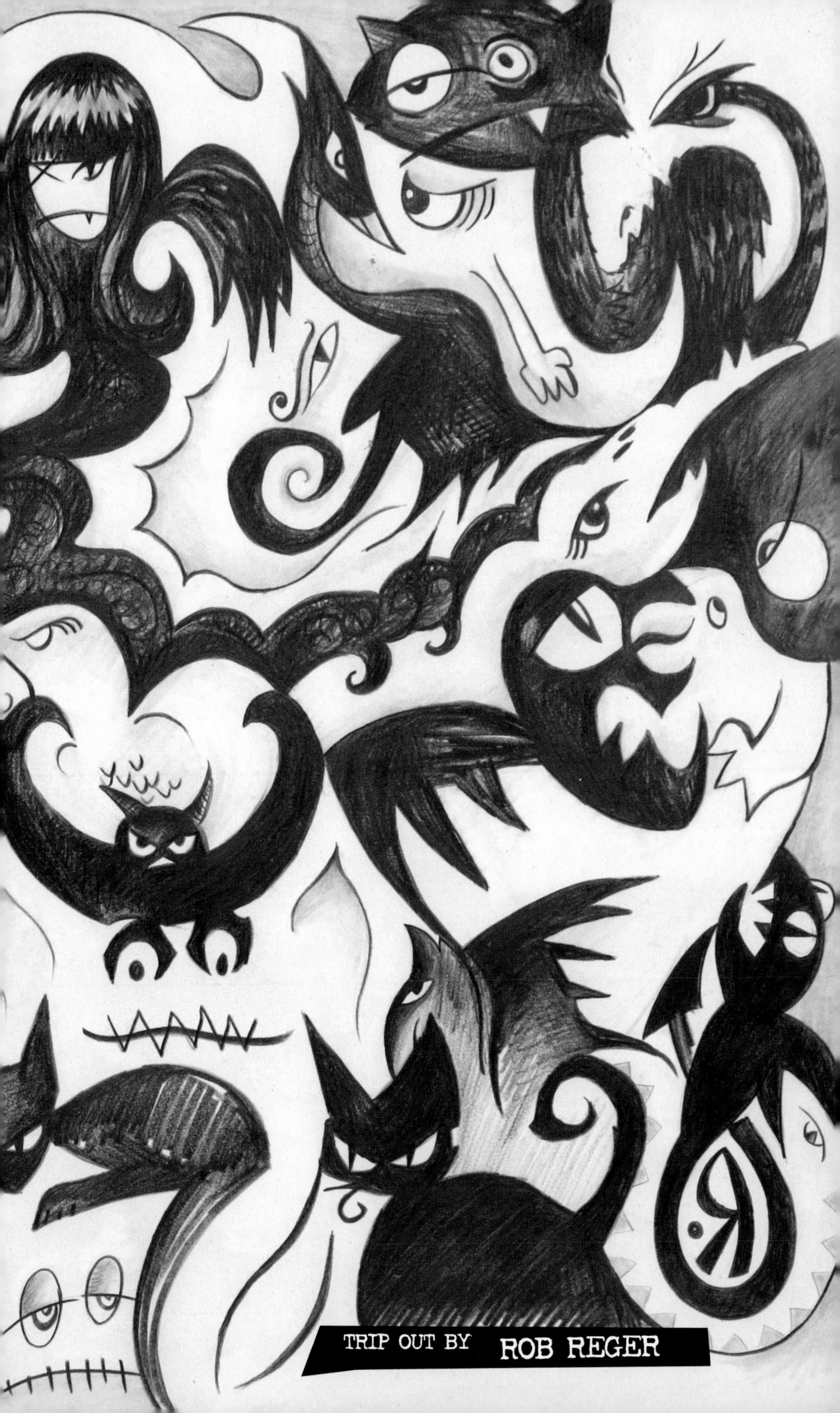
TRIP OUT BY ROB REGER

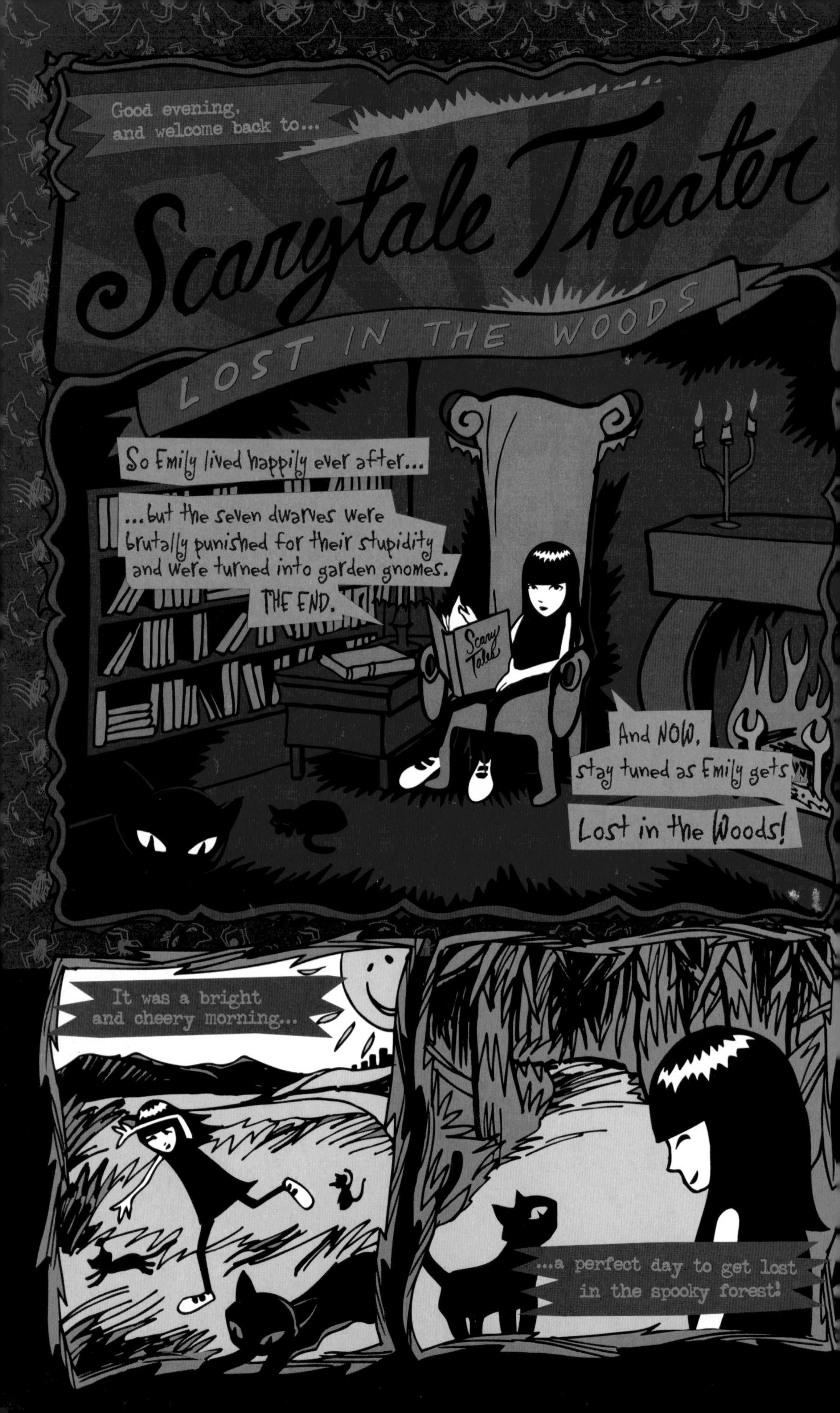

Good evening, and welcome back to...
Scarytale Theater
LOST IN THE WOODS
So Emily lived happily ever after...
...but the seven dwarves were brutally punished for their stupidity and were turned into garden gnomes.
THE END.
Scary Tales
And NOW, stay tuned as Emily gets
Lost in the Woods!
It was a bright and cheery morning...
...a perfect day to get lost in the spooky forest!

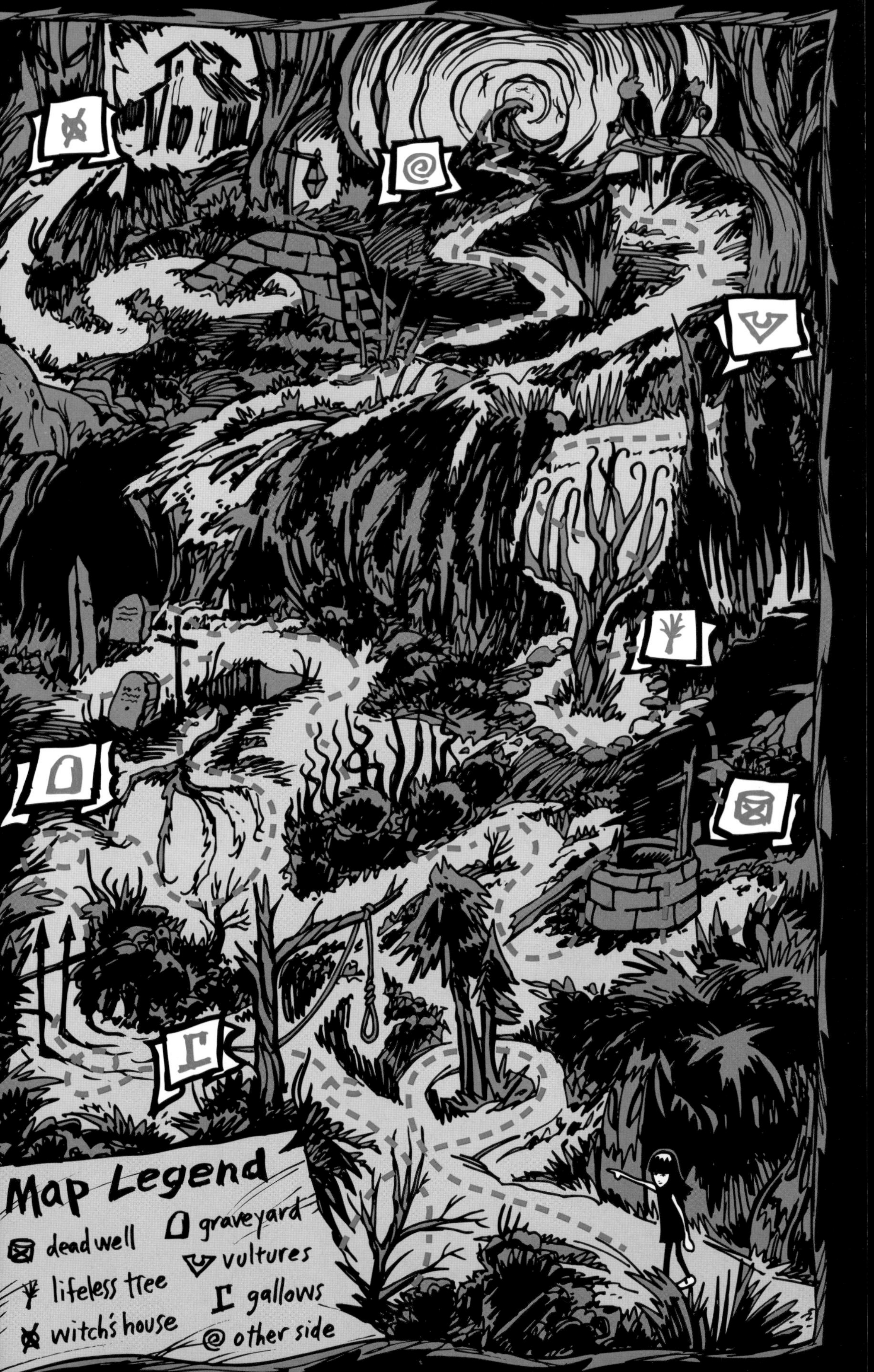
Map Legend
dead well
lifeless tree
witch's house
graveyard
vultures
gallows
@ other side

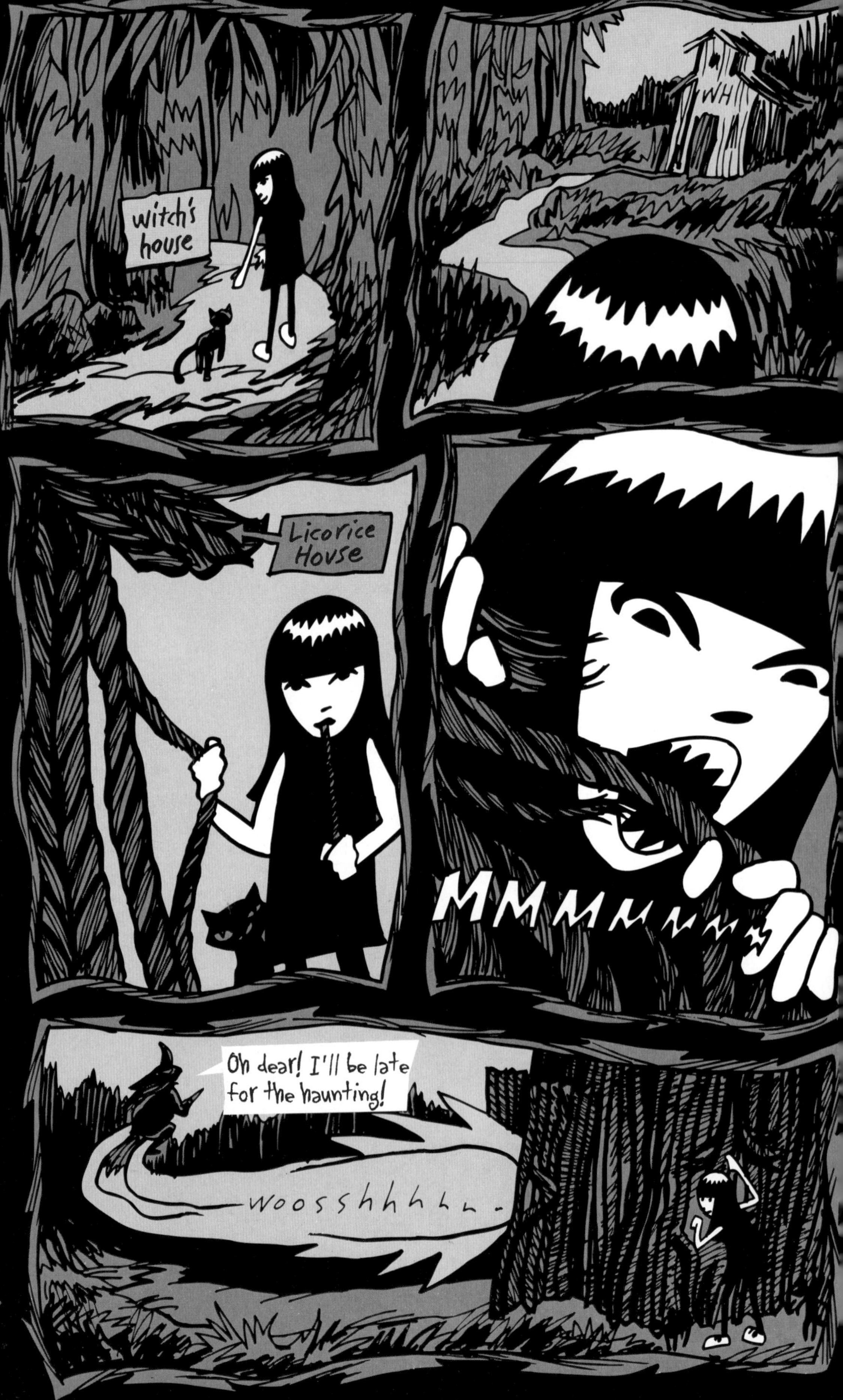
witch's house
WH
Licorice House
MMMMMMM
Oh dear! I'll be late for the haunting!
woosshhhhh..

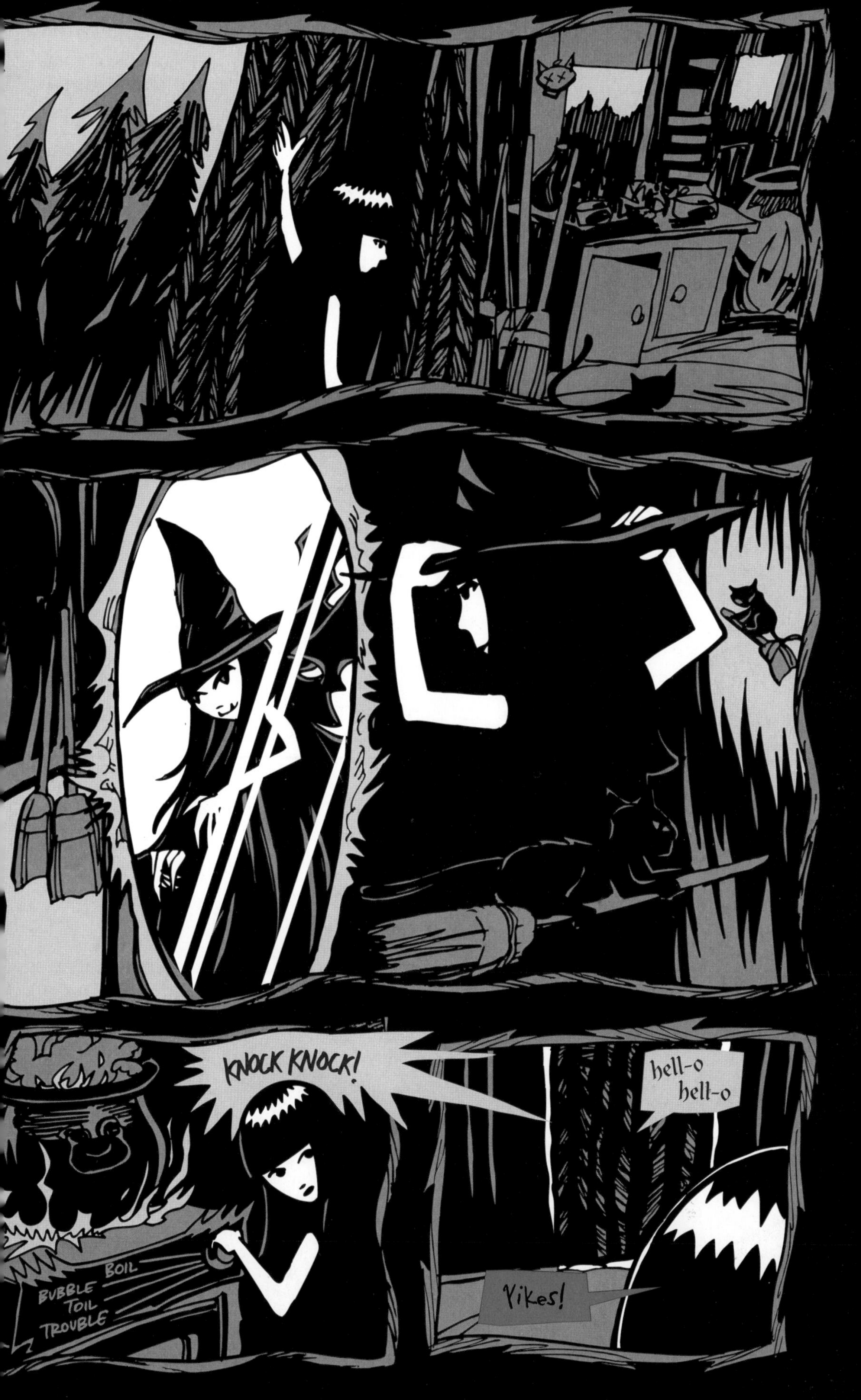
KNOCK KNOCK!
BOIL
BUBBLE
TOIL
TROUBLE
hell-o
hell-o
Yikes!

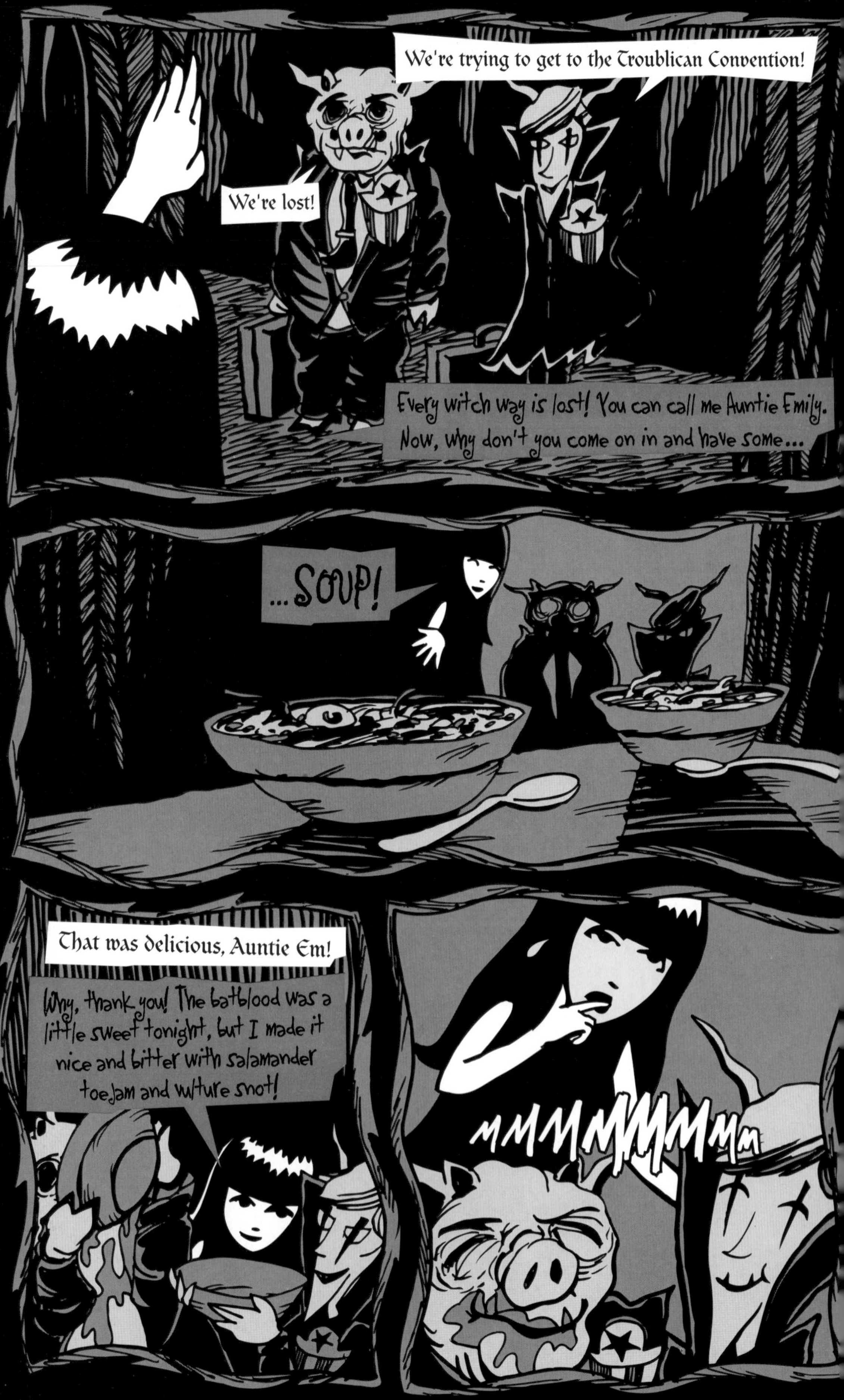
We're trying to get to the Troublican Convention!
We're lost!
Every witch way is lost! You can call me Auntie Emily. Now, why don't you come on in and have some...
...SOUP!
That was delicious, Auntie Em!
Why, thank you! The batblood was a little sweet tonight, but I made it nice and bitter with salamander toejam and vulture snot!
MMMMMMMMMMm

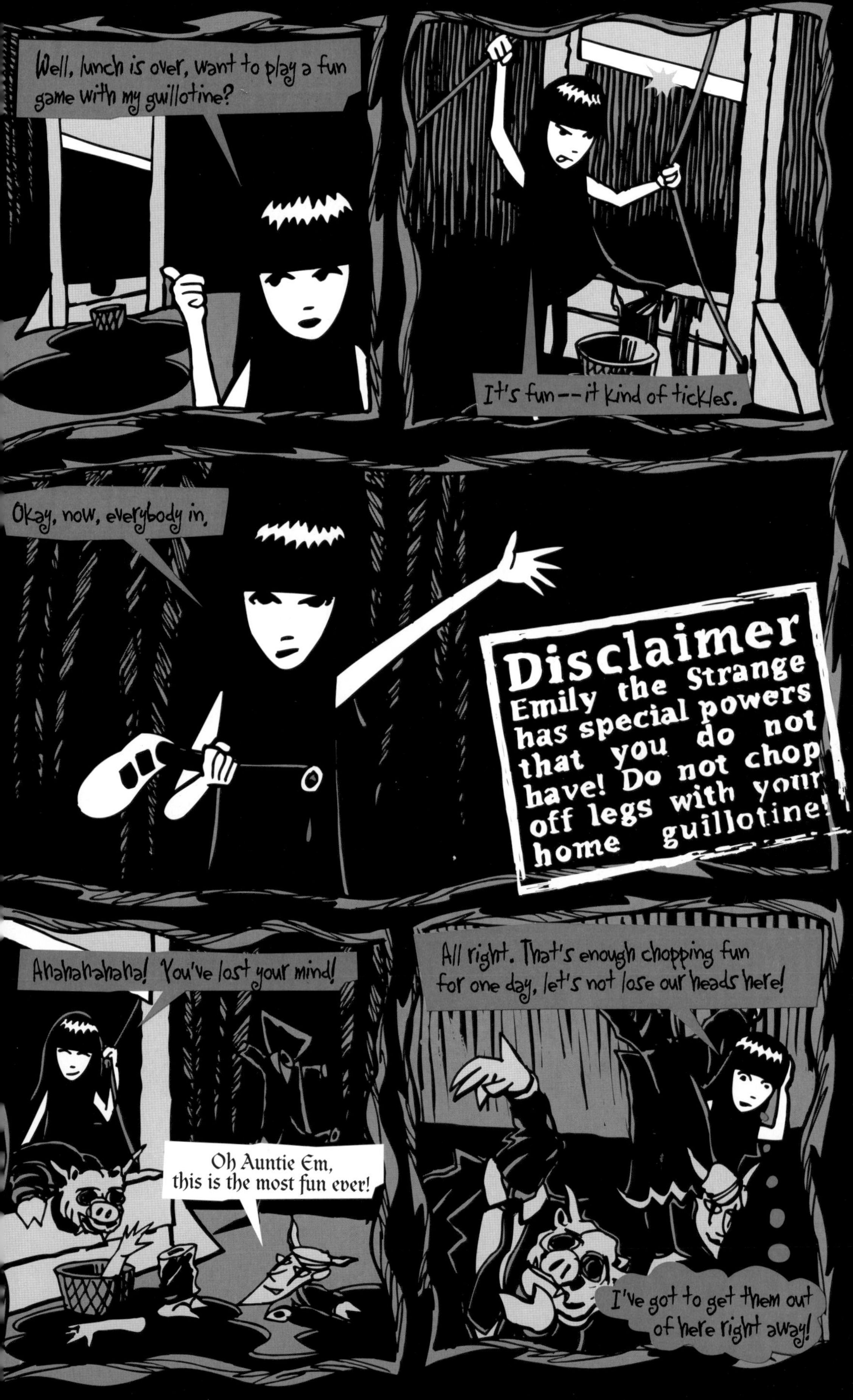
Well, lunch is over, want to play a fun game with my guillotine?
It's fun -- it kind of tickles.
Okay, now, everybody in.
Disclaimer
Emily the Strange has special powers that you do not have! Do not chop off legs with your home guillotine!
Ahahahahaha! You've lost your mind!
Oh Auntie Em, this is the most fun ever!
All right. That's enough chopping fun for one day, let's not lose our heads here!
I've got to get them out of here right away!

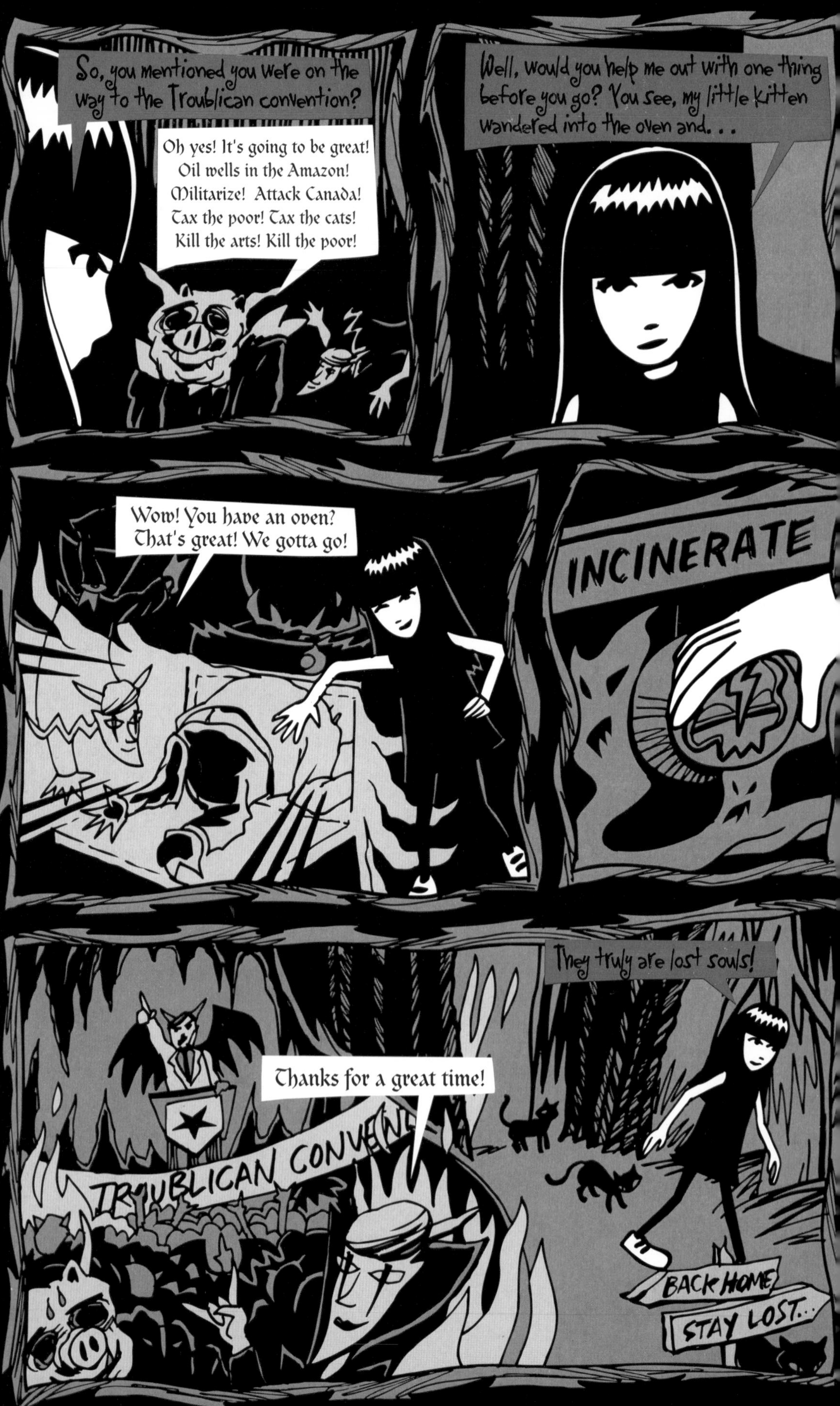
So, you mentioned you were on the way to the Troublican convention?
Oh yes! It's going to be great! Oil wells in the Amazon! Militarize! Attack Canada! Tax the poor! Tax the cats! Kill the arts! Kill the poor!
Well, would you help me out with one thing before you go? You see, my little kitten wandered into the oven and. . .
Wow! You have an oven? That's great! We gotta go!
INCINERATE
TROUBLICAN CONVEN
Thanks for a great time!
They truly are lost souls!
BACK HOME
STAY LOST. . .

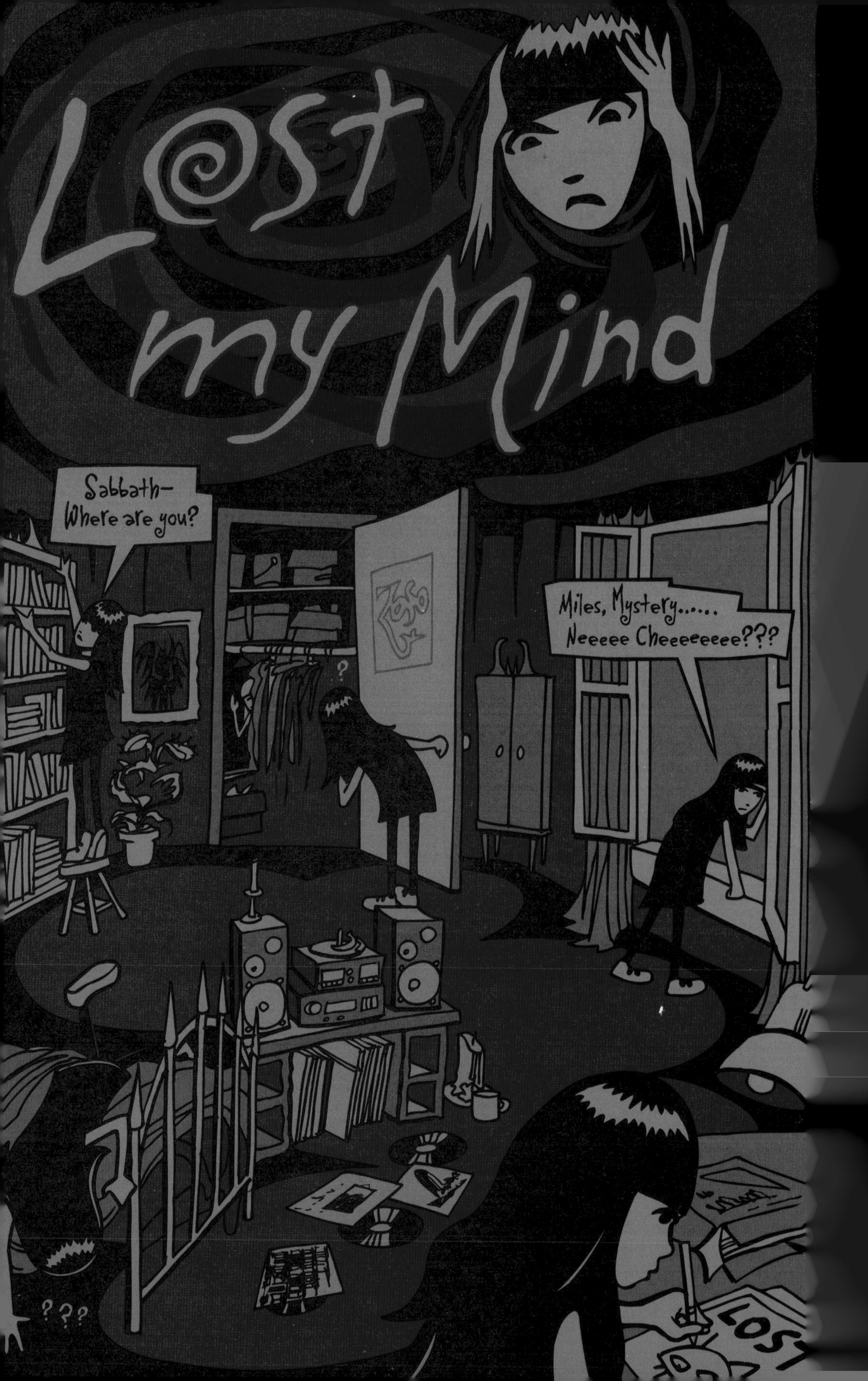
Lost my Mind
Sabbath—
Where are you?
?
Miles, Mystery......
Neeeee Cheeeeeeee???
???
LOST

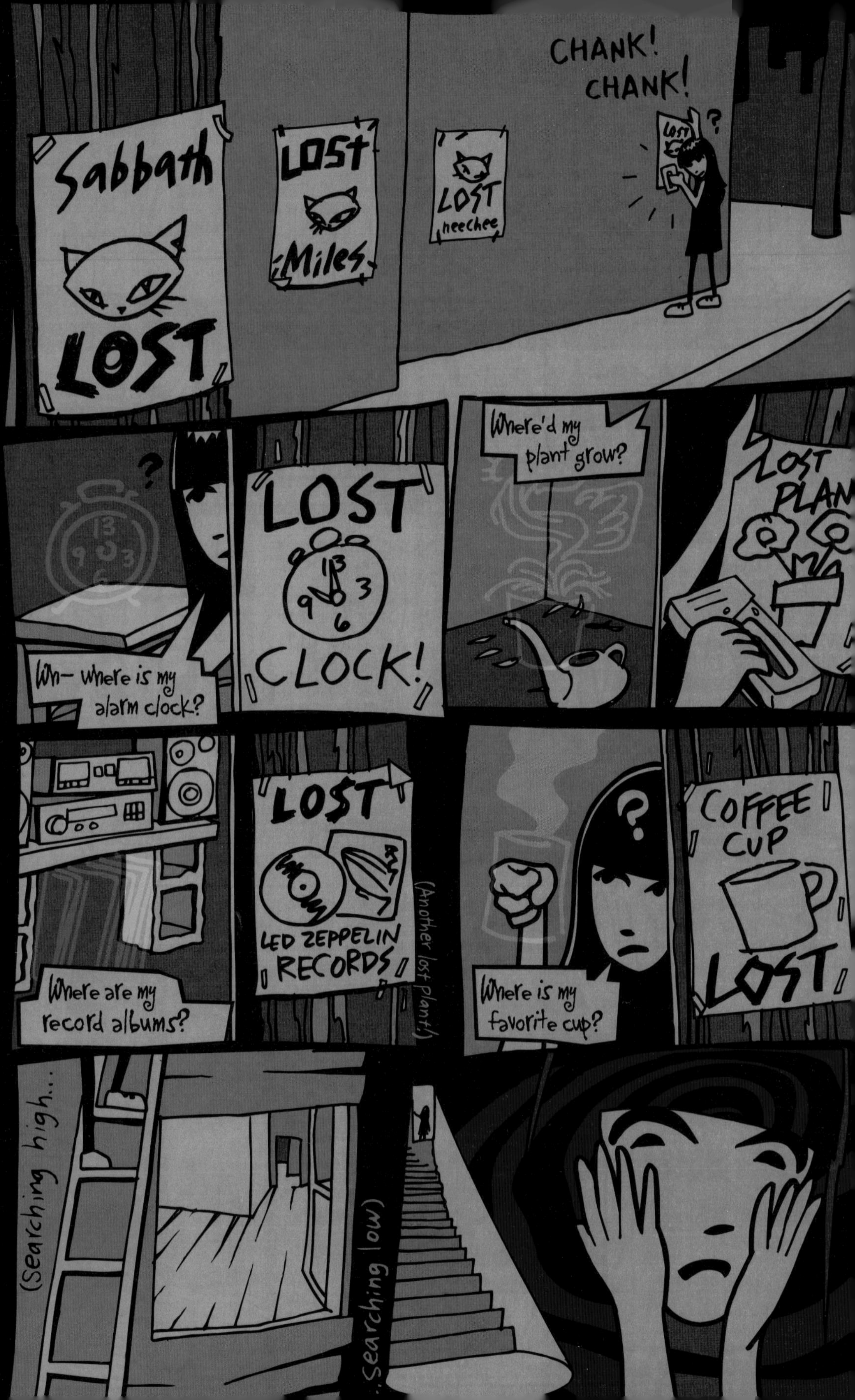

Sabbath
LOST
LOST
Miles
LOST
neechee
CHANK! CHANK!
?
LOST
?
Wh- where is my alarm clock?
LOST
CLOCK!
Where'd my plant grow?
LOST PLAN
Where are my record albums?
LOST
LED ZEPPELIN RECORDS
(Another lost plant!)
?
Where is my favorite cup?
COFFEE CUP
LOST
(searching high...
...searching low)

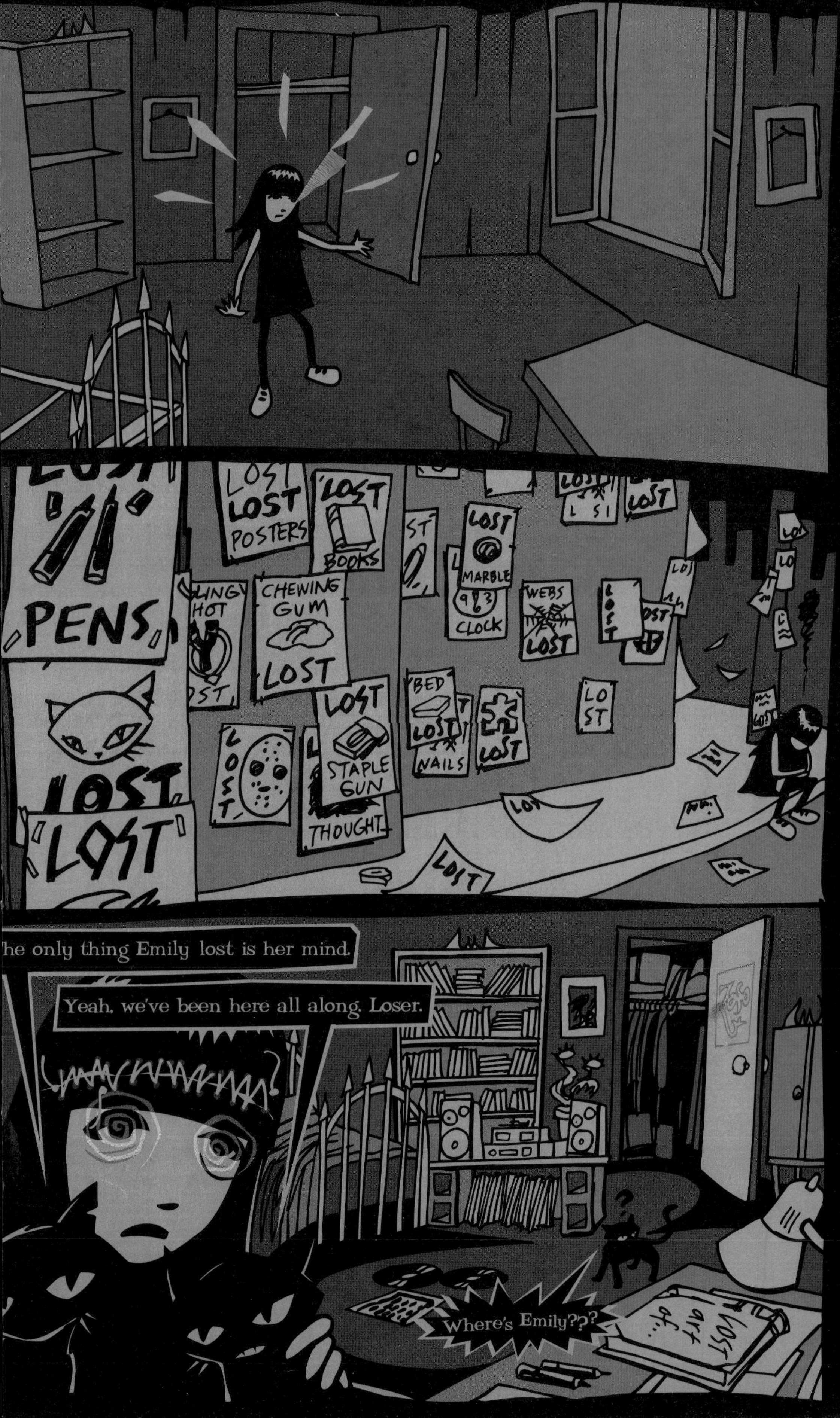
LOST
PENS
LOST
LOST
LOST
POSTERS
LOST
BOOKS
LOST
MARBLE
CLOCK
CHEWING GUM
LOST
WEBS
LOST
LOST
STAPLE GUN
THOUGHT
BED
LOST
NAILS
LOST
LO
ST
LOST
LOST
he only thing Emily lost is her mind.
Yeah, we've been here all along. Loser.
Where's Emily???
LOST art of...

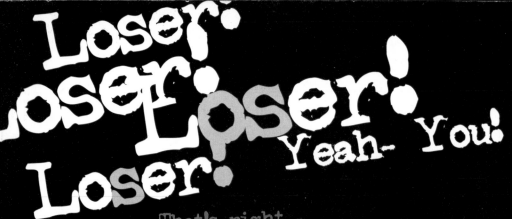

Loser! loser! Loser! Loser! Loser! Yeah- You!

That's right -
You are a loser, and we want to reward
you for it. Emily wants YOU to lose 9
challenges and win LOST PLACE!

1. Lose the Remote
- Permanently kill your TV! Break free of the idiot box
and prove it. Do something creative with (or to) your TV
and send us a photo or send us your remote.

2. Lose the Race.
- Enter a competition and come in last place. Send proof.

3. Lose your Marbles.
- Literally or figuratively. You decide! Send proof!

4. Lose your Lunch (or just your cookies)
- DO NOT SEND US VOMIT, PLEASE! - Just tell us about it.

5. Lose your Place in Line
- Wait in a long line, then leave when you get to the
front. Send a photo or get a witness.

6. Lose track of time
- Break your watch or spend a day without looking at any
clocks. Time is meaningless. Send your broken watch or
tell us how your perspective changed without keeping
track of time in 50 words or less.

7. Lose face
- Tell us your deepest, darkest most embarrassing secrets
in 50 words or less. We promise we won't publish names!

8. Lose your Cool
- Dork it up and turn it out! How uncool can you be?
Send photos or a story with a witness form.

9. Lose your Way Home
- Make a bad map and get lost yourself or send someone
somewhere else! Send directions and witness form from lost
person. Go to **http://www.emilystrange.com/beware/games/yafool/**
to download the YaFool map.

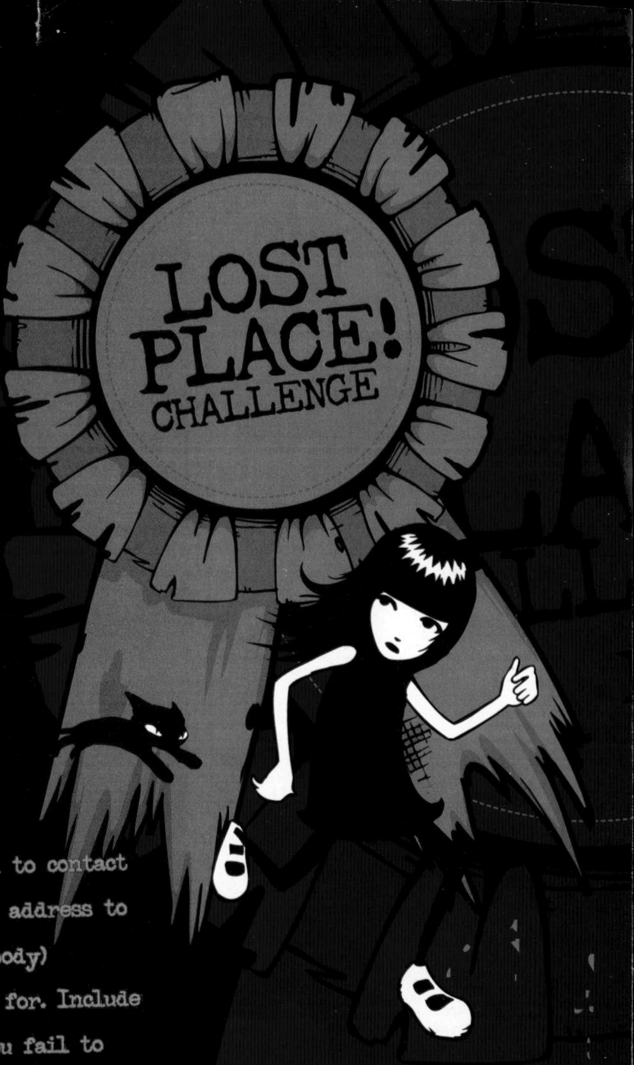
LOST PLACE! CHALLENGE

Losers win these prizes:

Complete 1-3 challenges:
Receive a special limited edition Emily Strange Lost Place sticker and Get Lost badge.

Complete 4-6 challenges:
Receive a Lost Place sticker, Get Lost badge and I'm a Loser badge.

Complete all challenges:
Receive a Lost Place sticker, Get Lost badge, I'm a Loser badge, Lost 4 Life badge and a
Lost For Life Ribbon!

DIRECTIONS:

1) Fill out the approval form completely. Please be sure to include your e-mail address and phone number in case we need to contact you regarding your submission. Most importantly - give us your shipping address to which we can send your loser loot! (Your info will NOT be given out to anybody)

2) Circle each category you are applying for. Include any and all proof of lostness required. Creativity and accuracy count here. If you fail to prove your lostness for the category, you will be denied.

3) Send your submissions to:
EmilyStrange.com/LOST PLACE CHALLENGE
970 I Street
Arcata, CA 95521 USA

LOST PLACE CHALLENGE brought to you by:

DARK HORSE COMICS

Emily the Strange

For printable forms and more info visit:
ttp://www.emilystrange.com/beware/games/LostPlace

r clip these out - or even photocopy them - whatever...
u don't wanna cut up your precious comic book- do you?

LOST PLACE approval form

__________ DATE

NAME: __________

ADDRESS: __________

PHONE: __________

EMAIL: __________

CIRCLE CHALLENGES applying for

1. Lose the Remote	4. Lose your Lunch	7. Lose Face
2. Lose the Race	5. Lose your Place in Line	8. Lose your Cool
3. Lose your Marbles	6. Lose Track of Time	9. Lose your Way Home

Include proof of worthiness for each on seperate sheets.

Send to: EmilyStrange.com/LOST PLACE CHALLENGE,
970 I Street, Arcata, CA 95521 USA

Witness Inspection Program

I swear on my own grave the acts in question happened exactly as stated. I will be forever unhappy and tormented if I bear false witness.

WITNESS SIGNATURE __________ DATE

The fine print: All submissions become property of EmilyStrange.com and we reserve the right to share any images or content on the website. If you want something back, we'll say we lost it! Submissions may also be sent via e-mail to lostplace@emilystrange.com. Cosmic Debris or EmilyStrange.com assumes no responsibility for the actions a person takes to earn Lost Place. Have fun but BE SAFE! Limit one entry per person. Entry deadline is June 30, 2006. Prizes awarded while supplies last. All entries are subject to Emily's approval. All prizes are available in limited quantities, so act quickly! Please allow up to 60 days for delivery. Now Get Lost Place!

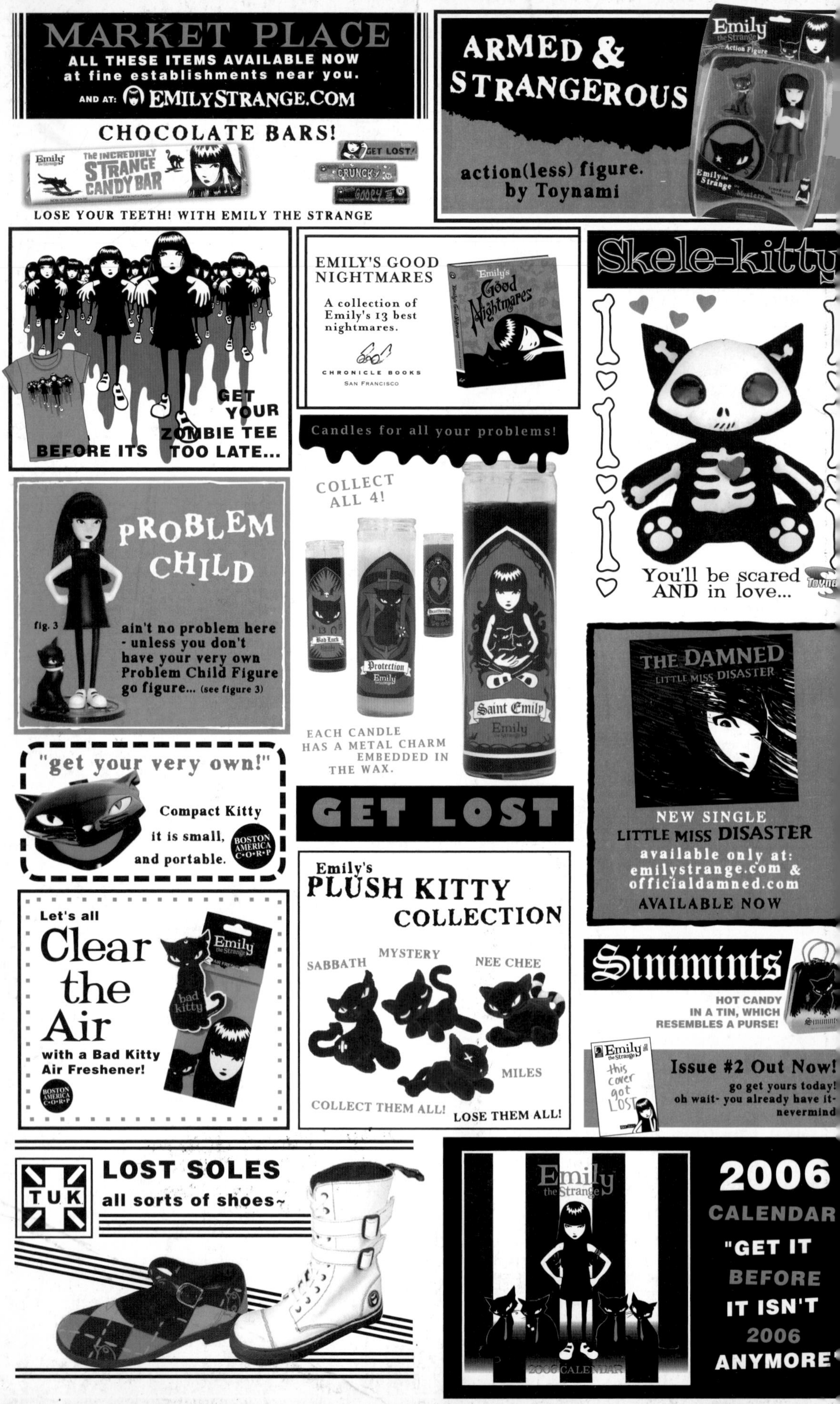
MARKET PLACE
ALL THESE ITEMS AVAILABLE NOW
at fine establishments near you.
AND AT: EMILYSTRANGE.COM
CHOCOLATE BARS!
Emily
THE INCREDIBLY STRANGE CANDY BAR
GET LOST!
CRUNCHY
GOOEY
LOSE YOUR TEETH! WITH EMILY THE STRANGE
ARMED & STRANGEROUS
action(less) figure.
by Toynami
Emily the Strange
Action Figure
EMILY'S GOOD NIGHTMARES
A collection of Emily's 13 best nightmares.
CHRONICLE BOOKS
SAN FRANCISCO
Emily's Good Nightmares
Skele-kitty
You'll be scared AND in love...
GET YOUR ZOMBIE TEE BEFORE ITS TOO LATE...
Candles for all your problems!
COLLECT ALL 4!
Bad Luck
Protection
Emily
Saint Emily
Emily
EACH CANDLE HAS A METAL CHARM EMBEDDED IN THE WAX.
PROBLEM CHILD
fig. 3
ain't no problem here - unless you don't have your very own Problem Child Figure go figure... (see figure 3)
THE DAMNED
LITTLE MISS DISASTER
NEW SINGLE
LITTLE MISS DISASTER
available only at:
emilystrange.com &
officialdamned.com
AVAILABLE NOW
"get your very own!"
Compact Kitty
it is small,
and portable.
BOSTON AMERICA C·O·R·P
GET LOST
Emily's PLUSH KITTY COLLECTION
SABBATH
MYSTERY
NEE CHEE
MILES
COLLECT THEM ALL!
LOSE THEM ALL!
Let's all Clear the Air
with a Bad Kitty Air Freshener!
BOSTON AMERICA C·O·R·P
Emily the Strange
bad kitty
Sinimints
HOT CANDY IN A TIN, WHICH RESEMBLES A PURSE!
Emily the Strange
this cover got LOST
Issue #2 Out Now!
go get yours today!
oh wait- you already have it-
nevermind
TUK
LOST SOLES
all sorts of shoes~
Emily the Strange
2006 CALENDAR
2006
CALENDAR
"GET IT BEFORE IT ISN'T 2006 ANYMORE"